DYNASTY WARS

Published by Dark Titan Publishing. A division of Dark Titan Imaginations and Products.

Cover art by Mary Landro.
Website: mlandart.com
Instagram: @mlandart
X/Twitter: @mlandartt

Hardcover ISBN: 979-8-9899434-3-2
Paperback ISBN: 979-8-9899434-5-6
eBook ISBN: 979-8-9899434-4-9

darktitanbooks.com

TY RON W. C. ROBINSON II

CHAPTERS

BOOK 11: HIDDEN WAR
1

BOOK 12: BATTLE OF THE UNIVERSE
37

BOOK 13: WAR OF THE UNIVERSE
89

HIDDEN WAR

PROLOGUE

The Citadel of Enchantment sat in an undisclosed landscape. Away from society and the continuous rush of living. A distant place where only silence moved through the air. One side of the landscape was lush and living with animals. The other was near desolate and almost a deep desert. Within the Citadel, Doctor Fortune worked inside his sorcerer's study while Huang remained in the library, reading through several grimoires. Tom Bradley, now known as Doctor Mysticism roamed through the Citadel, seeing a slot of doors which can transport others to foreign locations across the earth and beyond.

Fortune maneuvered his abilities. Holding up two orbs of magical energy. The one on his left was black as the night sky. The right one was blooming with a bright blue. Fortune sighed.

"Something's off."

The room began to shake without notice, catching Fortune's focus. He rushed toward the outside, seeing Huang coming from the library. They give each other a look with no answer. Tom stands near the entrance as Fortune and Huang reach him.

"What is going on?" Huang asked.

"Earthquake?" Tom wondered.

"This is not an earthquake." Fortune answered. "This is not even earthly."

The tremors increased and came to a sudden stop. The three waited as they hear footsteps inching toward the door. Ready for a fight, their sorcerer gear manifested upon them. Their hands glowed with magic. Prepared, the doors of the Citadel opened.

"Sorcerers." The visitor spoke.

"Who are you?" Tom said.

"He is the Specter Errant." Fortune said. "I must ask, why have you come to us?"

"I would not be here if it wasn't urgent and dire. The Holy Artifact of Life has been stolen from The T.I.T.A.N. headquarters."

"The Holy Artifact of Life?" Huang said. "The one from the books?"

"Yes." Fortune said. "It's been in the hands of T.I.T.A.N. ever since The Battle of Retropolis."

"And we didn't have it here?"

"Their leader refused to hand it over. I'm certain now they're thinking otherwise."

Fortune looked toward Specter Errant.

"Do you know who stole it?"

"It was Death. She infiltrated the headquarters with the assistance of Noldar and Kex Kendrick to retrieve the artifact. Where they are now, I cannot say. Their location is shrouded from my vision."

"We'll need to contact The Swordman." Fortune said.

"Why?" Huang asked.

"Because knowing him, he already has a trail on Death."

1

PROPHECIES

Judgedath, Centro, Europe. The Sky-Rapier swooped across the night sky over the city of Sinister Judge. Inside the craft was The Swordman, to his left was Commander Norland and to his right was Q-Arrow. All three focused on the mission. Flying beside to The Swordman's aircraft was The Nano Man, his nanosuit detailed with stealth, giving it a darker appearance rather than his traditional midnight teal and gold style.

"Where are those other guys?" Nano Man asked.

"They're already on the ground." The Swordman said. "Take a look."

Nano Man looked toward the ground and quickly sees a bolt of lightning crash from the sky near the entrance to the city. The Voltage has arrived. Next to him came Jack Stone, riding on a motorcycle. Behind him appeared John Terror with his own motorcycle. Landing from the sky in front of them was Dameon Mason, whom they've come to know as the Bionic Rage.

"Didn't know you were showing up." Voltage said to Rage.

"I came because The Swordman asked." Rage replied. "And how I could help others in this matter."

"My only question is how do we get past the gate?" Jack Stone pointed, seeing the size of the entrance gate.

Behind them, the Sky-Rapier lands and Nano Man with it. The Swordman, Norland, and Q-Arrow exited.

"We're here to infiltrate the V.A.U.L.T. base." The Swordman said. "Not the palace."

"Ok." Q-Arrow said. "And what if the Judge steps out from his palace and discovers we're here?"

"He already knows we're here." The Swordman noted.

The eight stare at the palace. Seeing its massive draw and detailed appearance. The eerie feeling of Judge inside bothered Q-Arrow, as he has never met Sinister Judge in person. Yet out of all of them, only Commander Norland has encountered him. The Swordman took out a map, an interior look into the V.A.U.L.T. building. Norland pointed toward the sections highlighted upon the map.

"The building is large, yet we can search the place and make our exit before the mass of their security discover us." Norland said.

"What's the plan?" Terror asked.

"We each split up into four teams. Search these four sections. One of them will have what we're looking for."

"And what are we looking for exactly?" Jack Stone questioned.

"The Holy Artifact of Life." The Swordman answered.

"I'm sorry. I don't know what that is."

"It's what caused The Battle of Retropolis." Nano Man said. "The source of the invaders' arrival."

"You're serious?" Q-Arrow asked The Swordman. "I thought that thing was in T.I.T.A.N.'s hands? How did it get stolen?"

"Death stole it. She managed to infiltrate their headquarters and steal the artifact."

"Alone?"

"No." Norland said. "Kex Kendrick and Noldar were aiding her."

"Great. This is sounding like our first team-up remember. Same artifact. same three villains."

"Are they looking to start another Battle of Retropolis incident?" The Voltage asked.

"Death's looking to release her brother." The Swordman said. "This time I believe she will succeed."

"Hold on." Nano Man said. "You believe Death will find a way to release her brother from his prison?"

"Yes."

The map was marked. Four teams. The Swordman and Norland. Nano Man and Q-Arrow. Voltage and Rage. Terror and Stone. Knowing their positions and directions, the four teams make their way into the V.A.U.L.T. headquarters. The tall gate was the entrance toward Palace Judge.

Within the headquarters, V.A.U.L.T. security is at large. Their hands on their firearms and batons. Some carried shields layered with kinetic energy. In the shadows of the nearby hall, The Swordman and Norland move with speed, yet with silence. In the development section of the headquarters, Voltage and Rage enter through an unlocked door. Taking them by surprise as they see only six armed men inside the room. Voltage turned toward Rage, who only shrugged.

"We can take them." Voltage said.

"True. But, we cannot make a notice on ourselves."

"I can take them out before anyone notices."

"They're not a problem." Rage pointed. "Our objective is to search this section for the artifact and leave."

Voltage sighed.

"True. True."

Taking Rage's words, they move quietly through the sector as the armed men remained in their conversation. Voltage couldn't make out their conversation as they spoke in Centronian. In another section of the headquarters, Nano Man and Q-Arrow find no soldiers. Not even any equipment.

"This place has been emptied." Q-Arrow said.

"Emptied fairly recently."

"How so?"

Nano Man emitted a light from his wrist, looking toward the floor, seeing tiremarks.

"They must've driven out of here before we arrived."

"Probably taken the artifact with them." Nano Man said. "We'll have to meet back up with Swordman. Give him the details."

"Let's get going then."

In the mechanical sector, Terror and Stone enter, seeing the technology within the room.

"This is what they make?" Stone said.

"That and more."

Vehicles of all sorts were in the sector. Used for the transportation of V.A.U.L.T. technology as well as travel for its soldiers. Before Terror and Stone could search the sector, the doors closed behind them, signaling their attention. They turned with haste, only to see Thunderstorm and Nicolas Jovano. Staring at them.

"These guys part of this group?" Stone asked.

"I don't think they are."

Back in the mechanical sector, The Swordman and Norland searched the main room, leading to the science sector. Within the sector, The Swordman could sense the presence of the artifact. Moving in haste while being unseen, he reached a closed room.

"It looks locked." Norland said.

"For the moment."

Taking out a device from his wrist, the small object broke the lock and The Swordman opened the door. Inside the laboratory stood a table. Atop the table, they could see fragments from an object. The fragments glowed with the touch of the light. They came from the artifact.

"It's gone." The Swordman noted.

"Where do you think they've taken it?"

"Could be anywhere." The Swordman replied. "Let's get out of here."

The Swordman contacted the others, stating to leave the headquarters and exit the city. While speaking, he could hear commotion. There's a fight going on. He and Norland make their move to reach it. The fight itself was between Terror and Stone against Thunderstorm and Jovano. Terror fired his guns toward Jovano, who only dodged them without fail. In Terror's eyes, Jovano disappeared and reappeared within mere seconds. Thunderstorm began to levitate as lightning emitted from his hands. Raising them, he began to fire down lightning bolts toward Stone, who ran and moved across the trucks.

"Didn't know you were skilled as a marksman." Jovano said.

"You know of me?"

"I do my due-diligence on all these heroes and villains."

"On which ones?"

"Ask Commander Norland as a start."

Meanwhile, The Voltage and Rage come into the sector, seeing the fight. Without fail, Rage lifted up his right arm, firing rounds toward Thunderstorm, striking him to the floor. Jovano looked over, seeing Rage and Voltage. He grunted before running out of the sector with an unnatural speed.

"You two ok?" Rage asked.

"We'll be fine." Terror said. "Where's Swordman and the Commander?"

"They said to meet them back outside." The Voltage said. "This place was a dud."

"Let's get going." Rage said.

Leaving the sectors, they reached the outside seeing Swordman and Norland. Voltage waved.

"They've made it." Norland said.

"And yet, not alone." The Swordman pointed.

Norland looked and saw Marion herself standing behind the other heroes. They noticed Swordman and Norland's looks and turned around seeing not only Marion, but Maveth, The Death-Bringer as well, surrounded by a pair of Judgedroids.

"Figured she would be here." Nano Man said.

"It's not a surprise." The Swordman said.

Marion began clapping as she stepped forward. Maveth remained still and quiet, yet his right hand was on his sword's hilt. His gaze was only focused on The Swordman.

"I didn't believe I would get the opportunity to see so many of you in one place. A spectacular affair."

"Where's the artifact?" The Swordman asked.

"Artifact? Which one?"

"You know."

Marion gave Swordman a look of clarity. She was aware of his words and knew the location of the artifact. She did not bother to tell him as Maveth stepped forward, his sword drawn out and pointed toward The Swordman. The Swordman himself drew out his sword.

"I've been waiting for a rematch." Maveth said.

"Seeking to lose again?"

"I did not lose our first encounter. It was only a draw in a matter of confusion."

Maveth was ready as was The Swordman. The other heroes knew what was about to take place as Marion took her leave. Maveth rushed toward The Swordman and the two clash their blades. Jack Stone ran into the fight to aid Swordman, yet Maveth's martial-arts skills proved him to be no match. Q-Arrow fired several arrows, which Maveth deflected with his sword. The Voltage fired lightning blasts toward him, only for Maveth to flip past them as they sparked into the pavement.

"Expected more from you." Maveth said.

"There's plenty more here." Voltage nodded.

"This guy's skilled." Nano Man said, observing Maveth's skillset.

Norland took a step forward and Maveth eyed him, ready for the challenge. Before Norland could make a move, Swordman raised his arm, signaling Norland to stop.

"Leave him to me. Prepare the craft for takeoff."

Norland nodded and turned away.

"Your fight is not with them, Danton. It's with me."

"You're right. However, I would never turn down the opportunity of facing the famed Canadian hero nor any of your allies behind you."

"You'll get that opportunity another time. Right now, it is between you and I."

"Very well, Swordman."

Maveth and The Swordman clashed their blades once more. This time, the other heroes made their way toward the exit. Terror and Stone leaped onto their motorcycles as Nano Man and Bionic Rage began to hover in the air. The Voltage charged himself up, sparking electricity across the concrete road. Q-Arrow and Norland enter the Sky-Rapier.

The sword fight continued with Swordman holding his own against Maveth. Neither of them have missed a step nor an attack. They moved with swiftness with their blades. The sparks from the impact only increased after each continuous strike. The Swordman noticed an opening and kicked Maveth in the abdomen before head-butting him. Stumbling Maveth as he regained his steps. Behind him walked the Judgedroids, eager to attack. Seeing Swordman outnumbered, Voltage bolted through the Judgedroids with such speed and ferocity, his electricity disintegrated the Judgedroids into ash. Maveth turned back, seeing the seared robots as he stared at Voltage.

"Told you there was plenty more." Voltage said with a scoff.

Maveth grunted in anger as The Swordman slammed his sword into Maveth's. the two struggled as Marion returned.

"Danton, we have to go!"

"Not until I finish this!"

"There's no time!"

Maveth looked into The Swordman's eyes. Seeing nothing but the white of them. No pupils in his sight. Maveth, with regret in his voice pulled back from The Swordman and turned away.

"We will find the artifact, Marion." The Swordman said.

"I'm sure you will." Marion smiled, turning away.

Sheathing his sword, The Swordman turned away and walked into his craft. The heroes made their leave from Judgedath, Centro.

2

A DARK WARNING

The raging blue flames surrounded the corridor of an ruined temple. Holding the flames at bay was Travis Vail, The Spirit-Seeker and by his side Gabriel Abraham, known to many as Abraham The Devilhunter. The flames, burning and searing the air around The Spirit-Seeker and The Devilhunter held in a trap, their target: The Sin Phantom. Vail and Abraham are not strangers to the Phantom, as they dealt with him during their first partnership.

"Looks like it's time for you to go." Vail said.

"I will never be gone!" The Sin Phantom shouted. "I am everlasting!"

"No." Abraham said. "You're not everlasting. You're only temporary."

Vail recited a word from his book and the flames consumed The Sin Phantom. Vanishing away into the smoke, taking the Phantom along with it. Vail sighed of relief and Abraham wiped the sweat from his forehead. Placing his book back into his coat pocket, Vail looked around, seeing the burned walls of the temple.

"Another job well done, eh."

"Yeah." Abraham said. "You think he's gone this time?"

"Maybe. Maybe not. We won't know for sure until the time comes. We could always as Shaw in case. He'll know for certain."

"We should find a way to communicate with him. Give him the details of this case."

"Right." Vail nodded. "So, what's next?"

Before Abraham could utter a word, a magical portal opened at the entrance to the ruined temple. Glowing bright violet with sparks of embers flowing across the corners. Stepping out of the portal was Doctor Fortune, nodding toward the two occult detectives.

"If you're here, something's wrong." Abraham said.

"A matter of dire need." Fortune said.

"How dire?" Vail questioned.

"The end of all things is at hand and our time to stop it is limited."

"What's happened?" Abraham asked.

"Come with me to the Citadel. I'll explain everything there."

Vail and Abraham agreed and followed Fortune through the portal.

Elsewhere, at the Clark Estate, The Swordman walked through his Swordlair as Taltus and Nano Man stood near the weapons desk. The Swordman approached them, laying his sword atop the desk.

"You know where she is?" Taltus asked.

"I don't. But, she'll make herself known. She can't resist attention."

"I could go around the city." Nano Man said. "Do a thorough search."

"You could. However, she's managed to shroud herself from technology. Not even my own tech can find her straightforward."

"What about me?" Taltus said. "I could do a search for her. Wherever she may be, Kendrick is with her. Just as Noldar."

"It's not that simple. Not anymore. She's taken the Artifact and no doubt, she's eager to release her brother from it."

The Swordman sighed, removing his hood and helmet. Taltus and Nano Man could see the distress in his eyes. He's never like this. Never.

"Kenari, what's going on?" Nano Man asked as his helmet opened.

"Something tragic is upon us. I've sensed it in the air for some time. I thought we would have more time, yet it seems we do not have enough."

"What are you referring to?" Taltus asked.

"Her brother's strength. Even though he's imprisoned, his power is growing. The only way for that to happen is to indicate the end is at hand. With his strength increasing even in prison, for sure he'll break free from the artifact. Even without his sister's help."

"What you're saying is even if we manage to find Death and retrieve the artifact, her brother might break free on his own."

"Correct."

"If this is as bad as you're saying, we'll need more of us." Nathan said. "As many heroes we can get."

"In truth, we'll need every last one of them."

"Where's Theus?" Nathan asked.

"He was dealing with some invaders back in Eragardia." Taltus said. "I only aided when I could. He said he'll be back to deliver the news on their victories."

"When he returns, make sure to deliver the news to him."

"I will."

In another part of the Earth. High above. A wormhole formed. Glowing dark violet and in the wormhole shined a bright flash of light. The light, near blinding shined and diminished within seconds. Where the wormhole once was, Darkous of the Astrals remained. His glowing blue eyes looked down upon the earth and around it. Even he, an Astral being could sense the growing power of Death's brother.

3

FUTURE MEETS PAST MEETS PRESENT

The Spellvector flew strongly across the time stream. The Champions of Destiny sat in the timeship. Crimson Mask, Ms. Titan, Jetlash, and their leader, Doctor Amadeus Omega. The ship reached a center point of location. Omega eyed it as he maneuvered the ship into its direction.

"Where are we headed?" Ms. Titan asked.

"Surprisingly, present day." Omega said. "Something's happening and it requires our assistance."

"I thought we were supposed to protect the time-stream." Crimson Mask said. "Why are we going into the present day exactly?"

"We'll find out once we arrive." Omega answered. "I know it isn't natural for one of our missions. But, this is something we cannot ignore."

The Spellvector flew through the portal and transported into the present day. Hovering over a desert as it made its landing. Upon the landing, the team exit and scout the surroundings.

"Where are we?" Jetlash asked.

"Present Day Arizona." Omega said.

"The signal led us here?" Ms. Titan asked. "In an empty desert?"

"Indeed it has."

While they walked, a gunshot fired. The Champions rushed toward cover with Jetlash using his armor tech to search the area. While searching, he caught the glint from a scope. Zooming in with his helmet's binoculars, he caught the sight of the sniper on a ridge in the distance. The sniper was Gunbaine.

"Over there!" Jetlash yelled.

Omega and the others looked, seeing the glint from the scope and behind Gunbaine appeared Maria Swan, G-Zero, Lance Gasper, and Lady Silvia. The Champions have been attacked by The Enforcement Order. Omega sighed with disgust.

"Who are they?" Ms. Titan questioned.

"Hired villains." Omega answered. "Never thought I would be facing them."

On the ridge, Gunbaine held his rifle steady. Taking slow breaths as Maria shouted behind him.

"Make sure you go for the head. No. the eyes. Yes! Go for the eyes!"

"Pipe down, Swan."

"Why are we hunting these guys down again?" Lance asked.

"A.B. informed us those guys are time-travelers. Not to be trusted."

"How can we be sure?" G-Zero asked. "Why not just asked them of their business."

"You want to present yourself in the face of time-travelers?"

"They might know something we don't."

"You don't say." Silvia scoffed.

On the other end of the desert ridge, The Champions began to plot out a diversion. Agreeing to the idea, Jetlash flew into the air, blasting energy beams toward the Enforcement Order. The villains moved from the blasts with Gunbaine firing shots back. Even Maria began to shoot with her handguns. Lady Silvia sighed, raising her arms as dark magic poured from his palms and quickly flew back toward the Champions, striking Jetlash in his chest, causing him to fall to the ground.

"Corbin!" Omega yelled.

"I'm fine. Just some pushback is all."

Omega grunted, pulling out his energy revolver.

"We have to stop them and get out of here."

"I agree." Crimson Mask said.

The Champions retaliated with their own attacks. The Enforcement Order moved from their previous location, searching for another. While on the move, Gunbaine looked down on his tracker, seeing two objects approaching their location. He gazed up and saw the two figures. One an android. The other engulfed in flames.

"Let's get out of here." Gunbaine said, looking at the two figures.

The Order make their escape as the two figures descend over the Champions. Omega looked toward them, recognizing them from the history books.

"Who are they?" Crimson Mask asked.

"The android is Ambush Bot." Omega said. "The one in flames, he's Flashburn."

"We have questions as to your arrival." Ambush Bot said. "Do you mind answering some questions for us?"

Omega looked toward his teammates and nodded.

"As long as we're able to go."

4

ERAGARDIA VISITATION

The kingdom of Eragardia shined with its glory. The greatness of the Eragardian gods reigned supreme, even during their most darkest days. Eragardia has remained to continued its mighty power after the War of the Thunder Gods. The Millennium God of Thunder, Theus flew over the streets of the kingdom. Theus' reputation had grown after the defeat of the foreign thunder gods, Zhor and Taraino. Theus arrived at the palace and greeted everyone he saw.

Inside the palace, Theus' father Eden stood firm, overlooking the kingdom. Theus approached him and also took a look out into the kingdom.

"Everything is well." Eden said.

"Yes, father. Everything is."

Eden turned toward Theus, sensing something.

"What do you have to say?"

"After the foreign gods came, I returned to Earth and saw it invaded by one of the Dark Gods. Myself and the heroes of Earth defeated him. Even Hadi was there on the dark god's side."

"Hadi. She was on Earth?"

"Aiding Oranos."

"Oranos invaded the Earth?" Eden said, taking a moment. "That is something of concern."

"Father, we defeated him and Hadi in his realm. Protected the earth from his grasp. There's nothing to worry about."

"Perhaps I've never told you about the Dark Gods."

"You once told me they were once in great power many eons ago. Until they were defeated by the Cosmics and a mortal who held an artifact."

"The Holy Artifact of Life." Eden said. "The artifact which conceals the chief of the Dark Gods."

"Negiter." Theus said. "You believe Oranos was trying to invade in order to break Negiter free?"

"No. It is prophesized that once Negiter is free, the end of all things shall commence. The fact that Oranos invaded the earth and Hadi aided him is only a sign of Negiter's growing power."

"What do you mean?"

"He's bound to be freed sooner rather than later."

A horn blew greatly from the kingdom's walls. Alerting Theus and Eden with haste as they rushed to find the source of the horn's call. Reaching the base of the horn, the Eragardian armies rallied themselves toward the entrance to the city.

"What is the cause of the horn?" Eden asked.

"Two unknowns are standing outside the gate. By the look of them, they're very powerful."

"I'll go have a look."

"Be cautious." Eden said.

"I won't be going alone."

Theus went to the outside and with him followed Lady Soya and the Mighty Trio. They reached the gate and Theus called for them to be opened. With slowness of speed, the gates opened, revealing Hadi and another figure. His skin as dark as the grass. His hair nearly as red as a burning sun. Wearing only what appeared to be pants as dark as the mountains. they stood tall over the likes of the Eragardians. Even taller than Theus himself.

"It appears we meet again, Millennium God." Hadi spoke.

"Goddess of Death." Theus said. "Why have you and your friend come to our doors?"

"We did not come here to fight. Yet. We've come to deliver a message to you and all Eragardia."

"And that message is?" Lady Soya asked.

The figure stepped forward. Gazing down at the Eragardians. He scoffed at their stature.

"I am Dranco. Dark God of Torment and Destruction and this day, I and Hadi proclaim the arrival of the Lord of the Dark Gods."

"The Lord of the Dark Gods?" Theus said to himself. "Who is this Lord your speak of?"

"He is mighty. He is powerful." Dranco said. "He is Negiter and he is about to return."

"And where will he return if I may ask?" Theus said.

"You should know, Millennium God." Hadi said. "He will make his presence known in the Earth. I think you should warn your companions there. Just in case he makes a spectacle of them."

Theus' hands brightened with lightning as does his eyes. Soya's sword was ready as the Mighty Trio were prepared. Even the Eragardian soldiers were set to battle with their swords, axes, and spears. Dranco could only let out a laugh.

"Don't jest with us, Eragardians. This day we will not have our battle. There's a time and place for everything."

Dranco turned away from the gates as did Hadi. She looked back toward Theus and smiled.

"Do warn everyone, Thunder God. The seasons have proclaimed the end is near."

Hadi and Dranco vanished through a rift in the air. Theus took their words to Eden and told his father all they spoke to him. Eden, slowly taking in the details prepared the army for the coming battle as Theus set out to return to Earth to warn his fellow allies of the impending danger that is to come.

5

UNITED ONCE MORE

While at the Clark Estate, The Swordman, Taltus, Nano Man, and Commander Norland continued to speak on the ongoing events. From the sky came the crack of thunder and in the front yard, Theus made his landfall. Theus entered the estate, being led by Allison Clark towards the Swordlair. Once he arrived, he saw his allies standing at the war table. Theus greeted them with hugs and handshakes.

"Weren't expecting you this soon." Taltus said. "What's happened?"

"You can sense it, can you?"

"Your eyes tell the story more than your words." The Swordman said.

"My realm was visited by two Dark Gods. One was Hadi, you remember her during our battle with Oranos."

"And the other?" Norland asked.

"Called himself Dranco. I've never encountered him nor heard of his feats."

"What did they want?"

"They came to proclaim the return of their leader. One called Negiter."

The Swordman nodded. Taltus gave him a look. As did Norland and Nano Man. Theus recognized their expressions. They know the name very well.

"Where is this Negiter?" Theus asked.

"Currently imprisoned in The Holy Artifact of Life." The Swordman said.

"Do you know its whereabouts?"

"We've been looking into that." Nano Man said. "All we know is that Death stole it from the T.I.T.A.N. headquarters."

"If only they listened to me, the artifact would be in this very room."

"You can't blame Colonel Nader, Kenari." Norland said. "He's only following his orders."

"Sometimes those orders must be changed to maintain structure." Norland nodded in agreement with Swordman.

"What do we do now?" Theus asked.

"We all go out and search." The Swordman said. "Death loves attention. Sooner or later, she'll make her location known."

The Swordman looked at the map on the table, seeing a blinking light upon Las Vegas. He pointed toward it.

"Meanwhile, there's somewhere I need to be."

Elsewhere at the Palace of Judge in Judgedath, Centro, Sinister Judge sat inside his throne room meditating on past events. More so the events that transpired during his short allegiance with Doctor Fortune against King Stroh The Conqueror and Celd. While Judge was meditating, a portal opened within the throne room. Judge's glowing eyes glare the portal and through the rift stepped Doctor Fortune.

"Hmm." Judge uttered.

"I do not come here to fight." Fortune said.

"You trespass on foreign soil. You know the cost of such actions."

"I do. Again, I am not here to fight. Only to discuss a matter."

"What kind of matter are you intending on discussing with Judge?"

"You actions regarding the Cryptic Zone. I know you're searching for a way to enter that realm."

"What I do is of my business."

"The Cryptic power is not something to be fooled with. You know this just as much as I."

"During our battle with the false Conqueror and Celd, we were aided by the stranger called Creed. I sensed the Cryptic Zone's power surging from him and through him."

"Creed didn't choose that power. It was granted unto him by the Cryptic Zone's lord."

"I will have a word with its lord. I will claim the power for myself."

"Judge, you can't."

"Judge does what Judge wants."

Fortune lowered his head in shame toward Judge's words. He looked at the ruler of Judgedath and nodded without emotion. Behind Fortune, the portal returned.

"I'll be seeing you, Judge." Fortune said, walking toward the portal.

Fortune entered the portal and it closed like lightning. Judge only stared. His stare became a glare. Slow breathing. Pure focus.

"Judge will have the Cryptic power. It is final."

The Vegas Strip is in a frenzy as Woodstalker had returned, summoning roots from the underground, ripping apart the streets. From the distance atop one of the buildings, slid down Q-Arrow. His arrow ready to be fired. Aiming closely, he fired the arrow. Piercing the chest of Woodstalker.

"Thought he would've learned by now."

Woodstalker ripped the arrow from his chest and immediately, the arrow exploded. Knocking the large creature down the street. Behind Q-Arrow appeared both The Swordman and Nano Man.

"Why are you guys here?" Q-Arrow asked.

Woodstalker arouse from the blast and charged toward the three heroes. The Swordman spotted him and leaped into the air, flipping behind the beast as Nano Man fired an energy beams from his palms, defeating Woodstalker with ease. Q-Arrow only sighed.

"I was going to take him down. I've done it before."

"I know." Nano Man said. "But, myself and Swords have come for a reason."

"I am aware. So, what is it this time? Found the artifact?"

"We're on the trail." The Swordman said. "That is why we're here. We need you to come with us."

"Alright. To where?"

6

FOUR SIDES OF THE PATH

The Resistance with Q-Arrow meet up with The Protectors. The two teams have found details regarding Death's location. A particular field in the outskirts of London, England. The Resistance and Q-Arrow take the decision of searching the field while The Protectors, being Fortune, Voltage, and Doctor Mysticism take the option of searching a wilderness location near Chicago, Illinois.

The Resistance and Q-Arrow arrived to the field in the London outskirts. Seeing a cemetery nearby. Nano Man scanned the area, finding no human being nearby. Taltus and Theus even scouted the grounds from the air, finding nothing.

"Something's not right." The Swordman uttered.

"What are you sensing?" Norland asked.

"There's something here. We can't see it however."

The Swordman raised his sword. Nano Man noticed as his energy palms began to charge. Norland knew Swordman would not raise his sword unless something was about to attack. The Sword began to glow. The light emitting from the blade moved through the grounds, eventually landing on a headstone a few feet away.

"What is that?" Q-Arrow asked.

"We're about to find out." The Swordman answered.

They moved quietly, entering the cemetery. Q-Arrow had his bow and arrow ready. Taltus and Theus hovered over the grounds. Norland was ready as his fists were set. They reached the headstone, finding nothing as the sword's light dimmed.

"Guess it was nothing." Q-Arrow said.

Behind him arose a ghostly figure, manifesting itself for visibility. The Resistance looked behind Q-Arrow, seeing the figure in full. Q-Arrow wasn't sure about their staring.

"It's behind me, huh?"

Q-Arrow turned, seeing the figure. In haste, he stepped back and aimed the arrow.

"Who are you?" The Swordman asked.

"I am Robert Shaw. The Ghost of England."

"Didn't know the country had a particular ghost." Nano Man said.

"We didn't come here to disturb you or the land." Norland said. "We're only here to find the artifact which Death has stolen."

Shaw stared. Thinking.

"She has taken The Holy Artifact of Life?"

"Yes." The Swordman said. "Our search for her and the artifact have led us here."

"I'm sorry to inform you, you're on a dead trail. Death has not ventured to these lands in recent memory."

"Great." Nano Man scoffed.

"But, you might know where she is?" Q-Arrow asked. "I mean you're a ghost and she's Death itself. It's not a hard calculation."

"I do not know where she is. Her essence has shrouded her locations from even the most spiritual of beings.:

"Do you mind coming along with us?" Nano Man asked. "We might be able to use your skill-set. If you have one, of course."

"You doubt my powers, mortal?"

"I don't doubt. Just not sure."

Shaw nodded with disgust and raised his hand, blasting Nano Man across the cemetery with only a gust of wind. Norland readied his fighting stance as Taltus and Theus came to the ground. Q-Arrow aimed his arrow. The Swordman remained still.

"Now, he will learn of respect. Even of strangers."

"We did not come here to fight." The Swordman said.

"You did not. I cannot say the same for your accomplices."

In the distance, a blue flame emerged. Forming a portal from the ground. Raising up from the searing flames were Travis Vail and Gabriel Abraham. Vail saw Shaw and nodded with a smirk before he looked and saw The Resistance.

"These are the heroes?" Abraham said.

"We are." Q-Arrow replied. "Who are you two?"

"First off, I am Travis Vail, Spirit-Seeker. This is my partner in the spiritual warfare, Abraham The Devilhunter."

"Devilhunter?" Q-Arrow said. "As in demon hunter?"

"Yes." Abraham said.

The Swordman walked over toward Vail and stared. Vail stared back and with a grin, the two shook hands.

"Good to see you again." Vail said.

"Likewise." The Swordman replied.

"You two know each other?" Norland asked.

"We were involved in a sort of mystery some time back." Vail answered. "Very short and simple case."

In the background of the meet-and-greet, Nano Man regained his footing and went over toward them, seeing Vail and Abraham. He was alarmed.

"There's more of these freaks?"

"Stand down, Nathan." Norland said. "They're not a threat."

"How can you be sure?"

"They didn't attack us."

"I can see that. Are they with the ghost?"

"Yes." Vail said, approaching Nano Man. "The Ghost is a friend of ours."

"Tell him to have some manners."

"He has all the manners, lad. It seems you do not."

"Enough." The Swordman said. "We are not here to combat one another. We came here in search of Death and the artifact. Nothing more."

"The artifact?" Vail asked. "Which ones do you speak of?"

"The Holy Artifact of Life." The Swordman answered. "Death has stolen it and we're on the hunt to retrieve it."

"If that artifact is opened, the end is upon us." Abraham said.

"We know that." Q-Arrow said. "Thanks for the retell."

"Any ideas as to where she and the artifact might be?" Vail questioned.

"So far, none." The Swordman said. "The recent trail led us here."

Vail thought to himself and looked toward Shaw.

"I might have an idea about that." Vail said. "First thing, we'll need Cindy."

Vail reached into his coat pocket, pulling out a card. He handed the card to Swordman and he looked upon it, seeing a map.

"Where does this lead?"

"To an abandoned church. Some said they saw Death there several days ago. Figured it's a best start."

The Swordman nodded, placing the map in his belt.

"You guys head to the church. Me and Abraham will pay Cindy a visit. She'll be of use for this."

"Agreed." The Swordman said.

He turned to the others and they left the cemetery. Vail and Abraham disappeared through another portal and Shaw vanished into the grounds of the graves. Above them with silence, The Visitant Outlander hovered. Watching them. Observing.

Elsewhere near Chicago, Fortune, Voltage, and Tom entered a base, quickly startling themselves as they saw ninjas. Voltage looked at their uniforms, noticing the claw marks on their torsos. They stare at The Warriors of The Claw.

"These guys again?"

"You know these ninjas?" Fortune asked.

"Unfortunately. Dealt with them sometime ago. Had more help than our numbers."

Fortune waved his hands, knocking the ninjas back with force. Instantly taking them out. Voltage remained paused.

"That was easy." Tom said.

"Thomas, do a search. See what you can find."

Tom nodded and levitated. Searching the base for anything related to Death or the artifact. While Tom searched, the sound of doors opening caught Fortune and Voltage's focus. Ready for a fight, they waited until the footsteps echoed through the base. Seeing the shadows on the floor, Fortune's hands glowed with magic as Voltage's body became consumed with lightning. The footsteps were from members of the Yonderers. Valinor, Crystalax, Gale, and The Surf. They stopped in their tracks seeing Fortune and Voltage.

"Nubreeds." Fortune said.

"Wait." Voltage said. "They're not the enemies."

"That's accurate." The Surf said. "And you guys are?"

"We're The Protectors." Tom said, landing on the floor.

"What did you find?" Fortune asked.

"Nothing. There's not even a magical presence here. It's all a dead end."

"For what it's worth," Valinor said. "Why are you three on our turf?"

"On a mission of importance." Fortune said. "An artifact was stolen and we're here to find it."

"Who stole it?" Valinor questioned.

"Someone you're not familiar with." Voltage said. "But, since you're here. Maybe you can aid us in finding it."

"Why would we?" The Surf said, holding water in his hand.

"Because this is your territory." Fortune said. "Who better than to show us the way."

Valinor looked at his teammates. Agreeing to aid them. Upon leaving the base, Dark Manhunter watched them from the rooftop. His eyes shined like a burning sun, yet unable for them to notice. Fortune paused in his steps and looked back, gazing up to the roof. He saw the Manhunter.

"Thus, the signs are commencing." Dark Manhunter spoke. "The times are at hand."

7

MAGIC AND SPIRITS

The Resistance arrived at the abandoned church told to them by Vail. A ruined structure. Appeared to have been burned down from the inside. The roof barely attached. The white walls scorched with burn marks.

"This the place?" Nano Man asked.

"It is." The Swordman said. "Let's get inside. See what we can find."

They entered the church. Easily getting through the broken doors. Within were only remains of pews. Half of them stood while the others were burnt. The scent in the air was only a memory of the incident. Nano Man scanned the area, seeing nothing. Although, he found something lurking in the air around the church.

"I'm getting something. But, my tech can't read the source."

"What is it?" Swordman asked.

"I'm not sure. But, I can guess it isn't a natural occurrence."

The Swordman raised up his sword with haste.

"Everyone prepare yourselves."

"What is it?" Q-Arrow questioned. "What do you know?"

"There's a spirit in this place."

"A spirit?"

"Swordman is correct." Theus said. "I can sense the presence of something otherworldly in the field. Like its lurking around this ruined place."

"Maybe it's a spirit of someone who died here. No harm there."

"No." Taltus said. "I'm getting a malevolent feeling. It's a darker play here.”

The church doors barged open with wind, startling the team. The Swordman held his sword steady as the wind swooped through the church like a traveler. The heroes remained calm. With each move of the wind, they did not move. The wind silenced and moved toward the front of the church. Hearing the wind slowing down, in front of them appeared Leta herself.

“Who the hell is she?” Q-Arrow said.

“She’s a ghost.” Nano Man replied.

“I’m not familiar with this one.” The Swordman noted. “Who are you?”

“I am the Lost Girl Spirit.”

“I think he meant a name.” Q-Arrow said.

“My name is Leta.” She said with a giggle.

“Why are you here, Leta?”

“To preserve the coming storm. The end is at hand and you’re in the way of it coming to pass.”

“She knows why we’re here.” Norland said. “What’s the move, Swordman?”

“Spirit, return to the realm where you came from.” Theus said. “Or else succumb to our might.”

“The only wrath that this church will feel is the fall of The Resistance.”

Leta went to strike them, until the sound of the church doors blasted open. Leta ceased from the attack, staring toward the entrance. Who she saw at the doors, she snarled with anger and hate. Standing at the door was Vail, Abraham, and Cinderella.

“Leta, dear.” Travis Vail said. “Why are you still lurking around old places?”

“After what you and that Sorcerer did to me, you believe I would just disappear from the living world?”

“Not really to be honest. Figured it best you did.”

“This is the Leta you told us about?” Cinderella asked.

“It is. Although, she’s lost a few steps along the years.”

Leta let out a loud shriek as she lunged to strike Vail. Knowing her tactics, Vail remained paused. Vail looked over to Swordman

“Swords, give her a slash will ya.”

The Swordman took his sword and slashed Leta, instantly evaporating her manifested body. The heroes were astonished by the attack. Vail shrugged his shoulders and smirked.

"Figured that would work."

"How did you know?" Norland asked.

"Swords' sword, if that makes sense, it's of a spiritual origin. Figured that could be used to remove her for the time being."

"So, she'll be back?" Q-Arrow said.

"Oh, hell yeah."

"She knew about everything." Taltus said. "She knew about Death and the artifact. It was all in her words."

Back in Chicago, Fortune, Voltage, and Tom walked with the Yonderers into the empty streets. They discussed past events and why the Protectors are in Chicago.

"So, you came all this way to find someone named Death?" Valinor said.

"Death itself." Fortune said. "She is Death itself."

"I see. And you guys believed she came through here with some kind of artifact?"

"The Holy Artifact of Life." Voltage said. "I think that's what it's called."

"We need to find her and the artifact immediately." Fortune said. "The entire universe is at stake."

"I'm sorry." The Surf paused. "What do you mean the entire universe?"

Fortune sighed. However, he understood the Yonderers have no knowledge on the spiritual events.

"The artifact she has stolen. Inside of it is her brother."

"Death has a brother?" Crystalax uttered.

"He once held this world under a dark rule. Ultimately lost it due to some interference from higher beings. Now, Death intends on releasing her brother from the artifact and setting him free in today's world."

"And you guys are looking to stop her from freeing her brother?" Gale said.

"Correct." Fortune answered.

Vainer looked at his teammates before turning back toward Fortune. With a nod, he had an answer to give.

"We understand. What if, we tag along with you on this mission?"

"I thought you guys have to deal with the remains of the ninjas?" Voltage said. "And that Rilla guy."

"We're not the only Yonderers." Gale said.

"There's more of us." The Surf added. "Back at the estate."

Fortune nodded.

"We'll take all the help we can get."

"Great." The Surf said.

"Ok, where do we start?" Valinor asked.

"Right now, we don't know." Fortune answered.

"I do." a voice echoed above them.

They gazed up into the night sky and descending from the darkness was none other than Darkous of the Astrals. His presence brought a touch of fear upon them, aside from Fortune and Tom.

"The Astral of Shadows." Fortune said. "We meet again.

"Doctor Fortune, Supreme Enchanter." Darkous greeted. "I know where Death remains."

"You do?"

"Go north. To Retropolis."

"Where in Retropolis?"

"The Castle."

Fortune knew of the castle, yet never traveled there. Knowing Darkous to be sincere, he took his word as he opened a portal to Retropolis.

"I need to inform The Resistance." Fortune said.

"Go to Retropolis." Darkous said. "I will inform them."

Fortune nodded as he, Voltage, Tom, and the Yonderers walked through the portal.

Back at the church, The Resistance found no sign of Death or any trace of the artifact. The Swordman became annoyed by the search.

"We need to go." Swordman said. "See what Fortune has found."

While they exited the church, Darkous was standing. The Resistance were somewhat startled, Vail only grinned.

"I'll be." Vail said. "Never thought I would see you again so soon."

"I can say the same, Spirit-Seeker."

"Another one?" Q-Arrow said.

"No." Vail answered. "This is Darkous of the Astrals. Before there were ghosts, there was his kind."

"Astrals." The Swordman said.

The Swordman approached Darkous, looking up toward him.

"I've heard of your kind." The Swordman said. "Ever since I was a child."

"Kenari Clark. The Swordman." Darkous said. "I've known of your lineage since its inception."

"Good to know."

"Darkous," Vail said. "I take it you know why we're here."

"You're looking for Death and the Holy Artifact of Life."

"You know where she may be?" Vail asked.

"I know where she is."

"Tell us." Swordman said.

"She's in the Retropolis Castle. She's expecting you."

The Swordman nodded, looking back at the team.

"Let's go. We'll need to contact Fortune and the others. Inform them of our move."

"Fortune is already in Retropolis." Darkous said. "He's looking for the castle."

"Did he find out before us?" Nano Man said.

"I told him. Right now, I will send you there, so you can regroup."

Darkous waved his hand, creating a portal to Retropolis.

"Death is not alone. For Noldar of Eragardia and Kex Kendrick of Enigma City are with her and they know you're all coming."

The Swordman took in his words.

"Understood. Let's not keep them waiting."

The heroes walked through the portal. Vail stepped last before stopping.

"I take it you'll be there?" Vail asked.

"I will. This is a universal matter."

Vail nodded.

"See you there."

Vail walked through the portal as it closed behind him. Darkous was already gone.

8

THE END OF AN AGE

The Resistance stepped through the portal, finding themselves in the outskirts of Retropolis. The Swordman moved with haste, knowing the land like the equipment in his belt. Vail gazed up to the night sky. Taking in the air.

"I remember the last time I was here." Vail said.

"Yeah." Cinderella said. "Feels like it was yesterday."

"And why were you two out here?" Nano Man asked.

"Searching for a mystery." Vail answered. "Ultimately found it."

"Where's Fortune?" Norland asked, looking around the field.

"He's around here somewhere."

"You're right." Cinderella said. "I can feel his magic."

"Would be better to see if it wasn't night." Q-Arrow said.

"True. But nightfall is where my work is best." Swordman said.

The Swordman turned to Vail.

"You know a way to contact Fortune?"

"I got just the thing."

Vail's right hand became engulfed in blue flames and he raised it high into the air, blasting the flames like a flare. The blue light emitted throughout the sky, far enough for the civilians of Retropolis to catch a glimpse of the glowing flame. Vail put down his hand, shaking off the fire.

"Give him a moment."

They waited and about three minutes later, a rift opened near them as Fortune, Voltage, Tom, and the Yonderers made themselves known.

Q-Arrow looked at the Yonderers, seeing their uniforms.

"Who are these guys?"

"They're nubreeds." Fortune said. "They're here to aid us."

"Didn't expect to see nubreeeds on my travels." Vail said. "This day is getting interesting by the moment."

"Yonderers." Swordman said. "Although, not all of you."

"You're The Swordman." The Surf pointed. "You actually exist."

"People are still on that theory?" Q-Arrow scoffed. "Yes, he exists. He's right there."

Now, I don't know where this castle is." Fortune said to Swordman. "But, I'm sure you do."

"I've been there before."

"When?" Nano Man asked.

"During my early years. Dealt with some vampires."

Voltage turned to Fortune and back at Swordman.

"What do you mean by vampires?"

"They do exist." Cinderella smiled.

"What he said." Fortune replied. "I'm following you."

The Swordman nodded.

"Follow me. The castle isn't far."

The heroes followed The Swordman down the path. Moving through the hidden roadway, in the distance The Swordman pointed. The heroes looked ahead and saw the castle.

"Taltus. Theus." Swordman said. "Give us an aerial position."

"Just what I was thinking." Taltus said as he and Theus flew toward the castle.

"We need a plan." Fortune said.

"Death doesn't work by plans." Swordman replied. "Chaos is her strategy."

Then what do we do?" Voltage questioned. "Just knock on the door?"

The Swordman nodded.

They approached the castle doors. Standing nearly twenty feet in height.

"How old is this place?" Q-Arrow asked.

"Centuries old." Swordman answered.

"And you fought vampires here?"

"Once."

"Weren't those vampires the same ones that invaded London some time ago?" Cinderella asked.

"You remember."

The Swordman approached the door and knocked. Stepping back, they waited for a response. Not even a minute later, the doors creaked open.

"That is creepy." Voltage said.

"I've had my fair share of creepy." Cinderella said. "It comes with the job."

"Let's find the artifact and get it away from here." Fortune said.

"Agreed." Nano Man added.

In the air, Taltus and Theus continued their scouting. Looking into the castle, Taltus could see Death, Noldar, and Kex Kendrick on the upper floor. The room was covered in technology. Mostly from Kendrick's company. Taltus signaled Theus and he looked, seeing the three within the castle. They flew down to the door as the others entered.

"They're at the top floor." Theus said. "Almost as if they're waiting for us."

"Who?" Fortune asked.

"Death, Noldar, and Kex Kendrick." Taltus answered.

"Let's reach that top floor." The Swordman said.

Taltus and Theus flew up through the castle towards the top floor as Fortune opened a portal, sending everyone immediately to the top floor. At the top, Theus slammed the door from its hinges. Taltus flew into the room, his eyes locked on Kendrick. Behind them arrived the heroes through Fortune's portal.

"They've arrived." Kendrick scoffed.

Walking up behind Kendrick was Noldar, wielding his spear. Theus stepped forward as Noldar held his hand up.

"Never thought I would see the Millennium God of Guile in person." Abraham said.

"Today is new for all of us." Q-Arrow said.

"You knew it would come to this." Noldar said to Theus.

"I've always known." Theus replied. "I figure it was you who gave the Dark Gods access into Eragardia."

"Someone had to make contact. Besides, it was all her plan."

At the desk behind Kendrick and Noldar was Death, slowly caressing the artifact. Swordman saw the artifact and quickly drew his sword. Death giggled at the sound of the blade.

"She's touching that thing like it's a love object." Vail said. "Very strange."

"Guys, there's no need for violence." Death spoke. "This is an exciting moment. We should all relish in his return."

"Your brother must remain imprisoned." Fortune said.

"Oh. The Doctor believes things will be better if he remains locked away. That's sad. For you, at least."

"Does she always dress like this?" Voltage said.

"Enough, Death." Swordman said. "Hand over the artifact."

"You know me, Swords. You know I won't."

"You leave us no choice. Retrieve the artifact. By any means."

"Ken," Cinderella said. "I can take her."

"I know you can. But we have to make sure the artifact stays intact."

"You don't have to tell me twice." Valinor said, twirling his staff.

The heroes rushed to reach Death and the artifact. Noldar and Kendrick intercepted with their own weapons. Noldar's spear deflected the projectile attacks while Kendrick raised up an energy shield to deflect their physical attacks.

"Always the tactic one." Noldar grinned.

"You've caused enough trouble for the last time." Theus said, blasting a lightning beam toward Noldar.

Taltus flew around Kendrick's force field, looking for a way to break through. The shield was made of other materials not known to Earth, Kendrick smiled as Taltus tried to punch through.

"Give up. Eventually, you tire yourself out. Giving me an easy victory."

"I never get tired."

Valinor took his own staff and twirled it, sucking in the force field. With his staff, Noldar spotted him and lunged with the spear pointed forward. Taltus rushed in and snatched Noldar by his throat, throwing him across the room as Theus caught him and slammed him into the stone floor. With another twirl, the force field evaporated, startling Kendrick as Taltus punched him in his chest, damaging his exosuit. Nano Man flew over him, using his own technology to shut down Kendrick's suit.

"Expected more." Nano Man said.

Noldar stood up and clashed with Valinor. Spear against Staff. Gale lifted her arms, brining into the castle her wind force gusts. Blowing Noldar and Kendrick back. The winds had no effect on Death. The Surf moved across the air on the water emitting from his palms. Crystalax transformed his body into pure crystal to deflect Noldar's spear beams. Emerald's eyes turned solid green as he let out a blast of energy, hitting Noldar in the chest, knocking him against the wall.

"You three are outnumbered." Fortune said. "Surrender."

"This battle you may have won." Kendrick said. "But, the war is about to begin."

With the fight taking place, Death watched. Holding the artifact closely. She stared and a smile grew on her face. Turning to the desk, she placed the artifact down and grabbed a hammer. Swordman looked and saw her wielding the hammer.

"No!"

"It's time, my brother." Death said.

Death raised the hammer as Swordman ran to reach her. Even Taltus and Theus' own flight speed was not enough to make the reach. The hammer was raised and crashed down upon the artifact, smashing it. The artifact exploded into a flash of bright white light. Nearly blinding everyone in the room except for Death. The explosion echoed all the way to the city. With the light dimming, smoke covered the room. Nano Man, using his helmet to see through the smoke saw Kendrick, Noldar, and Death were gone.

"Swordman." Nano Man said. "They're gone."

The Swordman remained silent as he looked over to the desk, seeing the fragments from the artifact.

"He's free." Fortune said with an exhale of worry.

Elsewhere, in the thick darkness of the night, Death's sinister laugh could be heard and it was silenced by something else.

"How long…?" A voice said in the darkness. "How long has it been?"

BATTLE
OF THE
UNIVERSE

9

CONSPIRACY REMATCH

The heroes exited the castle in haste. The Swordman received a signal from downtown Retropolis. The news is broadcasting Death's return. She stood in the middle of the streets, chanting her brother's name and his return.

"I need to get downtown fast." Swordman said.

Vail brought forth the flames again, opening a portal into downtown. The Swordman nodded as he stepped through. Before going in completely, he looked back toward the heroes.

"Contact everyone you know. Get everyone you know. The Battle of the Universe has begun."

The Swordman stepped through the portal and the portal closed. Vail looked at the others and smiled. Fortune opened a portal of his own as Voltage and the Yonderers came around him.

"I need to get back to L.A." Voltage said. "Have to make sure none of my villains managed to do anything in my absence."

"Good point." Fortune said. "I'll take you guys back to Chicago and Voltage back to Los Angeles. Me and Tom will return to the Citadel to find more information regarding Death's brother."

They exited through the portal, leaving Vail, Abraham, and Cinderella on the outside of the castle. Vail turned toward the castle, looking up to the top. Starting, he saw a shadow move. He nodded.

"Figured you were here." Vail said.

"Who are you talking to?" Abraham asked.

Vail pointed as Darkous manifested before them. Cinderella stepped back and Darkous calmed her.

"No need to concern yourself."

"Just the last time I saw you, you swooped in and helped us take down Gascoyne."

"It was a matter of urgency I could not ignore."

"And how come you didn't aid us in there?" Vail asked. "You could've stopped Death from smashing the artifact."

"I could not. The artifact, it carried a shield. A shield even invulnerable to my power."

"Really?" Abraham said.

"Negiter and I were created at the same time. Different roles. Different abilities."

"So, you've met this Negiter." Vail said. "Tell us something about him? Are we supposed to be fearful of this bloke?"

"Negiter is the chief of the Dark Gods. He is their leader. All the other dark gods pay obeisance to him. Unlike myself, a Astral being and a Spirit of the Darkness, Negiter holds no power over me."

"Because you're an Astral." Cinderella said.

"Yes." Darkous replied. "An Astral holds far more power than the gods." Vail nodded.

"So, what do we do now?"

"Take heed to The Swordman's warning. Contact everyone you know. Detectives, heroes, monsters, even this world's villains who are willing to do some good. With Negiter finally free, this world will take all it can to stand against him."

"I think we can get the group back together." Abraham said. "I'm sure we'll find a way to contact others."

"And what of you?" Vail asked Darkous. "Will you gather any forces to help this world?"

"I already have."

Vail smiled as he knew Darkous was telling the truth. Darkous turned away and evaporated into thick smoke.

"I need to get back to London." Cinderella said. "Contact some friends of mine to assist us?"

"Like who?" Vail asked.

"Red."

"Red?" Abraham said. "Like *Little Red Riding Hood*?"

"Yep." Vail answered. "What about you, Gabriel?"

"I'll speak to my students. See who else we can find back in D.C."

"Very well."

Vail opened a portal and the three walked through.

Back in Los Angeles, Voltage returned and quickly saw the city being attacked by Sonicwave. The last time the two battled, Voltage was nearly killed. This time Voltage couldn't hold back as he bolted through the streets of L.A., spearing Sonicwave with an electric force.

"I knew you would arrive." Sonicwave said.

"Where have you been?"

"Hibernating. An entity of my power must take time to grow."

"I cannot allow you to destroy this city. Not again."

"I'm not here to destroy this place. I'm here to give you a warning."

"A warning?"

"The dark gods have spoken. Their master is free and the cities of this world will bow before him or be destroyed. I am the least of your concerns."

"I still cannot allow you to go free."

"As if you have a choice."

Sonicwave stomped the ground, creating a tremor that knocked Voltage into the air. Using his static electricity, he caught himself and balanced his body in the air, impressing Sonicwave.

"You have skill."

"It's over."

"Not yet"

Sonicwave screeched and vanished from Voltage's sight. Once the screech cleared, Voltage took a look around the street, seeing some civilians laying on the road receiving help. In his mind, Sonicwave's words echoed. Dark days are indeed on the horizon. For everyone of the universe.

In downtown Retropolis, Death continued to shout praises of Negiter. The civilians moved away in panic. Vehicles drove down the roads in fear of being caught in Death's gaze. She looked up and from the sky, Swordman came. Landing on the road in front of her.

"About time you showed up."

"You destroyed the artifact."

"I did. It was time, mind you. His imprisonment was gonna come to an end anyway. You know the story."

"Not like this. There was a time appointed for it. You have forwarded everyone to the written words."

"Oh." Death paused. "You're right. I didn't think about that."

Swordman snatched Death by his coat and held her off her feet. She savored the moment. Taking it in.

"I'm taking you back to Pegasus."

"Um, as much as I would like that, it's not going to happen." Death said, pointing behind Swordman.

Swordman went to turn and was quickly ambushed. He fell to the pavement, dropping Death on her feet. Regaining his motion, Swordman looked up to see Dyclos, The Immortal Werewolf staring him down. Death laughed as she stood behind the brute beast.

"I have things to do, like greeting my brother."

"Death!" Swordman yelled.

"Don't concern yourself with her." Dyclos said. "We have a score to settle."

"The last time we faced each other, you were defeated." Swordman said. "Nearly killed."

"This time will be different. Only Negiter doesn't want you to die. Yet."

"He sent you here to weaken me?"

"No. He sent me to send a message."

"I need no message."

Swordman took his sword, slashing Dyclos' chest. The werewolf stepped back as Swordman went for another strike, only for Dyclos to deflect the blade with his claws. Snarling with anger, Dyclos lunged at Swordman, attempting to bite his head. Swordman dodged the coming bite and punched the werewolf in the face before kicking him in the chest.

"Ah." Dyclos said. "You're good."

"I know."

"We'll finish this another time."

"No we won't."

Swordman raised the sword, going for another slash, only to make an impact against… nothing. Dyclos was gone. Swordman remained alone in the streets of Retropolis. Surrounded by screams and passing vehicles. He sighed at the sights.

Elsewhere… elsewhere. Negiter dwelled in a secluded area. His long cape was as bright as the light. His eyes red as drenched blood. His focus was keen like a predator. Negiter looked, observing the entire world. Seeing the nations and their rule. He saw the people. Some happy and content. Others anger and displeased. He smirked.

"So much as changed. So much. I hope they are prepared for what I have to offer. An everlasting rule. Where all will be pleased. Where all will worship me."

10

THE CHIEF OF THE DARK GODS

Fortune and Tom returned to the Citadel, searching through the many books and scrolls within their libraries. Huang assisted them in the search, finding nothing much which spoke specifically of Negiter. Tom searched one of the shelves of the first library and discovered a scroll. Unrolling it, Tom saw the written words of a brief description of Negiter's reign. He took the scroll to Fortune, showing him the writing and the insignia on the bottom of the scroll.

"That's the same symbol The Specter Errant had on his chest." Huang said.

"It's the Mark of Helven." Fortune said. "A defining sign of Helvish power and might."

"Can we contact him?" Tom asked. "See what he knows?"

"I already know." Fortune said. "He told myself and the others after our battle with Oranos. He knew the symbol was from Negiter. A symbol from Negiter's dimension, Helven."

"Perhaps he knows something that can aid us in this coming battle." Tom said. "A way to win."

Fortune was unsure of The Specter Errant's involvement in the battle. As he was thinking, a knock came from the doors to which Huang walked and opened them. Seeing Darkous standing at their doorstep, Huang backed up with haste, feeling Darkous' Astral essence. Fortune and Tom walked over after hearing Huang's hard breathing. Reaching him, they saw Darkous at the door. Cloaked in his dark robe aside from his pale face, dark beard, and piercing blue pupils.

"Sorcerers." Darkous said. "May I enter?"

"You may." Fortune said.

Darkous entered the Citadel and the doors closed behind him without any aid.

"You know why I've come."

"I do." Fortune said. "Maybe you can enlighten us more on Negiter's history. So far, none of the books in this Citadel have any details on it."

"I will tell you all I know."

Darkous followed Fortune into the study where they sat down. Tom and Huang remained at the door as Darkous took the time to prepare to tell them what he knew. Fortune was ready.

"In the beginning, The Elohim created all things. He also created the Dark Gods. Beings who were designed to maintain the dark elements of the universe. Unlike them, he formed the Angels of the Spirit of Darkness, which I was the first."

"The Astrals." Fortune said.

Darkous nodded.

"In those days after The ha-Satan's fall and the fall of Man in the Garden, the Dark Gods were plotting to conquer the Earth. Negiter, being the first Dark God rallied his brothers and sisters into forming a coup to usurp humanity's rule and to claim the Earth as their own. For they could not rule the Third Heaven after witnessing The ha-Satan's fall."

"I must ask," Huang said. "You've met Satan himself?"

"I have. On numerous occasions. He's also aware of Negiter's return and I am certain he's plotting an arrival any time now."

"So, it's not just this Negiter we have to concern ourselves with," Tom said. "But, the Devil too?"

"Don't be bothered." Fortune said. "It was always going to come down to this eventually. Negiter was going to be freed anyhow. The prophecies spoke it."

Darkous looked toward Tom, seeing his youthfulness was clouding his mind.

"Do not let this bring you down, Thomas Bradley."

"You know my name?"

"I know everyone. It is my duty."

"There is one thing I must know." Fortune said. "How did Negiter become trapped in the artifact?"

"It happened during this world's Medieval age. In the beginning of the age, Negiter accomplished his long-term goal and conquered the world. Thus, forming the Dark Ages. He reign for years with terror and destruction. It was only until a mortal man who they called Harold Vosloo constructed the Holy Artifact of Life after receiving a dream. Once constructed, he brought the artifact out for everyone to see. With the artifact, Vosloo and many others of heroes, cosmic beings, and some gods alike fought back against Negiter and imprisoned him into the artifact."

"And he's been trapped in it until now." Fortune nodded. "Now, it's starting to make sense."

"Death has forwarded time by smashing the artifact and releasing him." Darkous said. "Everything the prophecies said was and is true."

"Even if the artifact wasn't smashed," Tom said. "Negiter was going to be freed anyway?"

"Yes." Darkous said. "Negiter plays a prominent role in the end of this world and the new one to come."

"It truly is the end of the world." Huang said with a sigh.

"The End of this World." Darkous noted. "And the beginning of a new world. A new universe."

"I have just one more question." Tom said to Darkous. "How does Negiter end?"

"The prophecies never spoke of Negiter's final end." Darkous answered. "It only mentions that he will come into battle against all forces. Good and evil. For Negiter's power nearly rivals that of The ha-Satan. If Negiter wanted to, he could take over all the dimensions if he desired. So far, he only wants Earth. As if it was made for him."

Fortune stood up from his chair after writing down everything Darkous told him of Negiter. Taking the information closely to the chest, Fortune suggested he finds The Swordman and informs him of the details. Darkous agreed and declared he would be present when necessary as all of the dimensions are preparing for the end.

11

THE SUPERNATURAL OCCURENCES

Fortune met up with The Swordman and informed him of all Darkous had told him. Taking the information to heart, Swordman knew they had to prepare in haste to face Negiter. Around the world, strange things began to take notice. Spirits roaming across cities in ways it had never been documented. Along with Swordman and Fortune were Nano Man, Travis Vail, and Gabriel Abraham. Vail read up on the strange activities and pointed toward one of them on the news site.

"Appears there's a familiar spirit lurking around one of the old churches in D.C."

"How familiar?" Fortune asked.

"Familiar to me." Vail answered. "I recognize it clearly. It's The Fog."

"The Fog?" Nano Man questioned. "You mean a fog?"

"It's a spiritual fog." Abraham replied. "A fog filled with spirits."

"That's a first for me."

"We need to find Negiter." Swordman said. "We know he's lurking around the earth. Somewhere."

"Then we should find a way to track down Death." Fortune said. "You know it just as much as I do. We need her to trace down Negiter."

"You're right. But the only way to find her is to-."

"Track down all this spiritual encounters." Vail said. "I know. It's my workplace."

"First thing's first." Swordman said. "We head to this church and stop whatever this Fog is doing."

"Very well then." Vail said. "Let's go."

They prepared to leave as Nano Man approached Vail.

"Did you by any chance contact any of your allies?"

"Mr. Nano Man. I did in fact speak to several of them. Don't worry, they'll arrive when the time is necessary."

"The time is now."

"They know when to make their mark. They move on a different clock. Unlike the rest of us."

"Where's Cinderella?" Fortune asked.

"She's doing some research back in London." Vail answered. "It appeared there were some supernatural activities happening even there."

"She can handle herself." Swordman said. "She's come when she has the time."

"See, Swords gets it." Vail said, pointing toward Nano Man.

"As I already known." Nano Man scoffed.

They prepared themselves and left for Washington D.C.

Back in Chicago, John Terror and Jade Horror ride their motorcycles down the streets on the outskirts of the city. Nothing but an open road ahead and behind with wide open fields surrounding them. They passed by the old building which was used for Agency X, the same building where Terror fought Hunter Vazquez. While riding, red mist encompassed the road in front of them, causing them to stop.

"What is that?" Jade asked.

"I'm not sure."

Terror stepped from his bike as did Jade. The two stood still as the red mist hovered. The stench of sulfur began to consume the air around them. Knowing the familiar scene, Terror was on alert. Inside the mist, Terror could make out two distinct shrouded figures. Terror shoved his trenchcoat and raised his pistol.

"Show yourselves."

The figures appeared paused. Until the mist moved and they stepped through it. Revealing themselves, brining a shock toward Terror and

Horror. They were staring at demonic versions of themselves. Terror held his pistol steady at his demonic doppelganger. Jade took out her knives.

"What are they?" Jade asked.

"They're demonic reflections of us. I met mine some time ago."

"You've met that thing before? When?"

"When we came back into each other's lives."

Jade stood silent.

"Now, yours? I've never encountered that one."

"Let's put them out of their misery." Jade said.

Jade ran toward her doppelganger, which screeched at her and lunged. Terror walked toward his doppelganger with his pistol in hand. Shooting toward its' head. The rounds of the pistol did little to affect the demonic being. Terror sighed, placing his pistol in the holster.

"I remember how I took you down."

Terror pulled from his trench coat's side a shotgun. The demonic doppelganger roared at him as Terror pulled trigger, blowing the head off the demon. He looked over, hearing Jade screaming as she pummeled her demonic counterpart until the demon was nothing but ripped fragments of charred meat on the pavement. She exhaled slowly. Calming down and she looked toward him. He shrugged his shoulders.

"Are they dead?" Jade asked.

"Dead? No. just out for the moment. Otherwise, my doppelganger would not be here."

"You're saying you killed it before?"

"Yes. With a shotgun shot to the head. The fact it returned proves to me, it will return."

"So will mine." Jade noted. "That's just great."

Terror nodded.

"It's not just happening here." Terror said.

"How do you know?"

Terror looked up into the air. He knew something was wrong.

"I'm not sure. But, something has happened. Otherwise, we wouldn't have run into them."

"Alright, we should get back to the others. Inform them of what's happening."

"Agreed." Terror said.

The two jumped onto their motorcycle and road away. As they rode into the distance, their demonic counterpart began to take shape. Reconstructing their bodies and they rose up. Standing still, they walked backwards into the returning mist.

Taltus, Norland, and Theus monitored several maps of Enigma City and the surrounding areas for anything out of the ordinary with the Fortress of Cytron. On the maps, the heroes found there were plenty of matters to attend which were not ordinary.

"These things are all spiritual." Theus pointed. "The energy around these places. I've seen them."

"It's lingering in the air." Norland said. "Even I can sense it."

"So far, Enigma City isn't having any issues." Taltus noted.

Taltus turned toward Norland and Theus. Within a second, a horn blew as the map flashed. Taltus turned to see two strange objects nearing Enigma City.

"Now there's something." Theus said.

"You two ready?" Taltus asked.

"Indeed." Norland answered.

The three heroes moved out toward Enigma City. Once they arrive, they found the civilians running in fear. Looking ahead, Taltus could see two figures. One upright and the other on all fours. Theus stared, seeing the four-legged being.

"What is that?" Norland asked.

"I do not know." Theus said. "I've never seen the like."

Taltus stepped forward as the civilians fled. Leaving the three heroes and the two strangers near the city's entrance.

"Name yourselves and state your business." Taltus commanded.

The upright man was covered in tattoos from head to toe. The four-legged beast snarled with its enlarged dog-like head and fire-red body. The monster gave off the stench of sulfur as its saliva burned the pavement with each drop. The man stepped forward, extending his arms.

"Greetings. I am The Ink Man. This is Satanic."

"Ink Man? Satanic?" Taltus said. "I do not know either of you."

"We know you, Protector of Enigma City." Ink Man said. "We were warned about your power. You and your two compatriots."

"Warned by who?" Theus asked. "Was it Noldar?"

"I've never heard of this Noldar. Our boss works in high places."

"Is it speaking of Negiter?" Norland wondered.

"Perhaps." Taltus said. "Until we know for certain, we maintain focus."

Taltus took another step forward as Satanic growled toward him.

"It would be best for you and your "pet" to turn around and leave this city."

"Oh, we will be leaving. After we've done our task."

"And your task is?"

"To bring you low. Until death is your desire."

Satanic ran toward Taltus, tackling him. Taltus held his own against the demon dog's strength as he lifted him up and tossed him back to the road. Theus and Norland stared at Ink Man as he only stood still. His eyes closed as he sat down on the pavement. Crossing his legs and raising his hands. He began to recite a chant and his tattoos began to peel from his skin, manifesting into physical beings. Tattoos of a bear and a tiger.

"His tattoos have a life of their own?" Norland said.

"Indeed." Theus said.

The bear and tiger rushed toward Norland and Theus. With Theus taking on the bear and the tiger striking with its paws at Norland. On the other end of the road, Taltus battled Satanic. Punching the demonic being with no effect. Norland kicked the tiger before holding it down and freezing it with his hands. Theus grabbed the bear and flew high into the air, holding the bear with one hand, Theus summoned lightning and burned the bear into fragments of ink. Ink Man looked and only sighed. Not out of bitterness or anger. But of nonchalant. He did not care. Theus landed, staring down Ink Man.

"Now, it is your turn." Theus said, pointing.

"Is it?" Ink Man questioned calmly.

Norland froze the tiger into a solid form of ice. He looked over and yelled for Theus. Theus flew over and smashed the tiger. The ice had melted quickly, only revealing ink on the road. Ink Man saw the melting ice and sighed once more. Taltus continued to battle Satanic, eventually using his lightning vision to slow down the demonic dog. Satanic fell down from the shock. Taltus, Norland, and Theus approached Ink Man, who's still sitting down.

"Stand up." Taltus said.

Ink Man did not move. Nor did his eyes open. Taltus reached down and grabbed Ink Man by his left arm, commanding for him to stand. Ink Man's eyes opened, glowing red as the sun and from there came an explosion. Blowing the three heroes back with force. Covering themselves from the blowing smoke. Taltus looked and found both Ink Man and Satanic gone from the city's entrance.

"Where did they go?" Norland asked.

"I do not know." Taltus said.

In Washington D.C., the team of heroes, sorcerers, and detectives had arrived. Coming to the old church, which Vail began to make a joke as to how many churches are being haunted by the spiritual beings. Abraham looked around the area.

"I've been hear before."

"When?" Fortune asked.

"One of my earlier investigations. I faced a cult of Hastur worshippers in this place."

"That's what happened to Hastur." Fortune said. "I heard about the encounter. You did good."

Vail looked toward the ground, seeing the beginnings of fog raising.

"Everyone stand alert." Vail said. "The Fog is coming."

They each prepared for The Fog. Nano Man's energy palms brightened. Swordman noticed.

"Those will not work."

"How do you mean?"

"They're spirits, rich fella." Vail said. "They have no physical attributes."

Nano Man grunted as the spirits of The Fog began to manifest. Swordman saw them, seeing American Civil War uniforms. Others had the apparel of medieval knights.

"Are they always dressed like this?" Nano Man asked.

"The Fog is a collection of spirits across many lands." Vail answered. "So, yes. They always look like this."

The Fog grew in size, surrounding the heroes. Fortune's hands glowed with energy as Vail conjured his fire. Before they could make a strike against the growing Fog, The Fog itself was blown away as if by a powerful force. Vail looked up, seeing Darkous descending. He nodded with a smirk.

"I didn't know you had that kind of power."

"The Fog is only in the way of important matters." Darkous said.

"Why have you come to us?" Swordman asked.

"I am certain Doctor Fortune has informed you all of what I've told him."

"He has." Vail said. "Tell us, like Swords said, why come?"

"I've come to warn you. Negiter's power is growing and I cannot find him. Even with the sensing of his power, I cannot track him down."

"What about Death?" Swordman asked.

"She herself is shrouded by his power. All of the Dark Gods are."

"You're saying you can't find any of them?" Fortune asked. "Any of the Dark Gods?"

"I cannot. For Negiter or someone of great power has shrouded them from even my prying eyes."

Fortune thought.

"Could it be The ha-Satan?"

"What?" Nano Man said.

"He's involved in this too?" Abraham said. "Seriously?"

"I figured he would be." Vail said. "He always is."

"Do you know where he is?" Fortune asked.

"Last I heard, he was roaming the earth. There's no telling where he might be."

"That's not great to hear."

"I will search the cosmos for him and anything that connects to Negiter. Right now, you must search the earth for anything you can find. I will always be around."

Darkous vanished into darkness. The heroes agreed to continue to follow the supernatural activities in search of clues to Negiter or any of the Dark Gods.

12

KINGDOMS AND STRANGERS

Over in Las Vegas, Q-Arrow began investigating the supernatural occurrences in his own territory. With help from Shadow and Cry-Slasher. Having heard the stories of ghost sightings through the city, Q-Arrow knew it had something to do with Negiter's freedom. Upon coming near the Vegas Strip, Shadow Hardy caught the glimpse of floating skulls in the air. Pointing high at them, Q-Arrow fired his arrows, destroying them.

"What are they?" Cry-Slasher asked.

"I've seen them before." Q-Arrow said. "Back in Chicago when I aided our other allies against a crazy ninja group with claw mark logos."

The skulls reappeared before them, Q-Arrow continued his rounds of shots, destroying the growing skulls. Until they ceased in the air and turned into dust. Unsure as to what happened, they look ahead, seeing a moving patch of smoke coming toward them. Shadow Hardy was set for the fight as was Cry-Slasher. Q-Arrow recognized the moving smoke. He too ka step forward with calmness.

"I know who you are." Q-Arrow said. "Show yourself before I make you."

Through the smoke came forth Sinister Fear. Cloaked in his dark robe with only his skull-like face showing. His broad shoulders gave the appearance of a horrifying striking appearance.

"You thought our battle was over?" Sinister Fear said toward Q-Arrow.

"I remember those words. However, it wasn't just me that defeated you back in Chicago. You should bother the others before coming to my city seeking to restart your little plans."

"I go where I am led."

"And who led you here?" Hardy said.

"The Lord of The Dark Gods. His power covers all the earth. His essence is bringing forth the spiritual aspects which have been lost. His power brought me here to Vegas. To give warning to those who will heed his words."

"His words?" Q-Arrow said. "Are you now his prophet?"

"I believe myself to be a speaker to his rule. Negiter will conquer this earth. All will submit to his rule."

"Did he talk like this when you last met?" Cry-Slasher asked.

"Not like this. He mostly spoke of himself. Something's different."

Q-Arrow raised his bow.

"Return to your city. Never come back."

Sinister Fear let out a laugh before backing up into the growing smoke.

"You will regret not taking heed, heroes." Sinister Fear said. "You shall see me again."

Through the smoke, Sinister Fear was gone. Leaving Q-Arrow, Hardy, and Slasher standing in confusion. Q-Arrow wasn't fazed by Sinister Fear's words as he and the others returned to their home base.

The city of Atlantis remained silent amidst the ongoing spiritual events taking place upon the surface. The Atlanteans themselves were aware of the recent events as Kular The Aqua-Barbarian told them of the artifact's ongoing activities. The Atlantean guards at the entrance gate began to notice strong tremors in the distance ahead of them. Sensing the tremors aren't coming from beneath the sands. The guards held their spears in preparation as the tremors continued to increase. Looking ahead, they rallied out the signal to the armies. The stairs of Atlantis became consumed with the coming Atlantean solders.

"Ready Yourselves!" The General screamed.

The army prepared for the battle. Kular came from the palace, seeing the army ready for battle. He grabbed his trident and headed down to his soldiers, standing in the front. Nodding toward the General.

"Anyone know what it may be?" Kular asked.

"We don't, Sire." The General said.

"Looks like we're about to find out."

The ground quaked until the two figures emerged from the distance. Running toward the Atlantean army were Dranco and Thrudhawk, the elite general of Oranos. Thrudawk roared with his beast-like appearance, wielding his double-axe staff. Dranco held no weapons. His hands were all he needed as the rushed through the army. Kular striking Thrudhawk as the two battled with their weaponry. Dranco fought the army on his own. Towering over them in height. He roared with every punch and kick he delivered. It struck Kular with confusion as to how the two could breathe underwater. thru hawk slammed his staff against Kular's trident, pushing him into the sand.

"Why have you come to my city?" Kular asked.

"We come in obedience to Negiter." Thrudhawk said. "Atlantis will be his to rule."

Pushing with great strength, Kular shoved Thrudhawk with his trident.

"Negiter will not have Atlantis!"

Both battled continually while Dranco easily took out most of the army. He savored the killing. His eyes glowing orange after every kill. His body giving off a shine of a glowing emerald. Thrudhawk noticed Dranco's increasing berserker behavior.

"Dranco! Do not kill them all! Negiter will have use of them!"

Dranco stomped the soldier into the sand. Taking slow breaths, he turned as Kular came forward with a strong strike to his face with the trident. Dranco fell as Thrudhawk went for another strike. Kular spotted him and raised his hand toward him, firing a bolt of lightning. Stumbling Thrudhawk.

"We need to get out of here." Thrudhawk said. "Inform Negiter."

Dranco glared toward Kular. The two stared down one another. Dranco shook his head, calming himself.

"Yes. We shall go."

Dranco and Thrudhawk fled from Atlantis, moving with great speed. Kular contained himself as he aided the remaining soldiers. Afterwards, Kular informed his people he will return to the surface to gain more information on the two strangers and the ongoing events happening to the earth.

13

TITAGOD WARFARE

Taltus continued his watch over Enigma City. Seeing no sign of Ink Man or Satanic. Even the enemies he's faced in the past had not been seen since their encounter. Taltus nodded as he turned away from the city looking to return to his home base. While flying out of the city, a sonic boom exploded above the city, grabbing his attention. Stopping mid-flight, Taltus looked over the city, seeing a portal open. Through the portal came forth a legion of soldiers, clad in ruby red armor. Behind them appeared someone in their similar uniform, and yet had a commanding presence. He descended upon the city.

"I seek the one you call Taltus! The Titagod who roams over these lands!"

Hearing the call, Taltus flew toward the legion and their commander. The commander looked up to the sky as Taltus made his landing. The legion armed with weapons stood for a fight. Their commander held his hand high, his legion remained still.

"It is about time we meet." The commander said.

"You summoned me." Taltus said. "Who are you and your army?"

"Allow me to introduce myself. I am Lord Damos of Titanon. I am a Titagod."

Taltus was silent. He always believed he was the only titagod. Now, he stands in front of another.

"I thought I was the only one." Taltus said.

"For someone who was banished at birth, you have no idea to your race." Damos said. "For there are plenty of us on Titanon. Zeus banished you to this world because he knew you would rebel against his rule. Some of us obeyed his word. Such as I and from that, I became the leading General of not only Titanon, but of Mount Olympus itself."

"You work with Zeus?"

"Absolutely. It was his idea that I make myself known to you since you unleashed the Dark Gods' lord upon the earth."

"I will not allow Zeus or Negiter to take over this world. Not while I'm here."

"Then, Son of Hypernon. You will have to die."

Damos commanded his legion to attack Taltus. They moved with a swift strike. Attacking him with their energy guns and staves. Taltus deflected the attacks and blew past the legion. Striking them while flying through their pack. Damos stood impressed by Taltus' choice of retaliation. Taltus knew the legion did not have his abilities. They were simple Olympians in armor.

"Now, it is time you face a real challenge." Damos said. "From a real Titagod!"

Damos struck Taltus, tackling him through the streets and into the buildings of Enigma City. Taltus struggled to gain strength, managing to kick Damos from him. Taltus turned and attacked Damos with punches, knocking him into the air before collapsing him into the ground with an axe-handle attack. In the crater, Damos arose. Grinning. He savored the fight. Taltus and Damos took more rounds at one another. From a series of blows to the head, to even a lightning vision beam-battle which Damos overpowered Taltus, backing him into a wall.

"You have heart." Damos nodded. "I will give you that. But, you don't use your anger wisely."

Damos went for another attack, this time a stomp. But, before he could make the strike, a gust of wind knocked Damos back from Taltus. Shoving him into the pavement. Taltus arose from the wall and looked, seeing another figure standing over Damos. It was a woman wearing a similar uniform to his own switching the white for silver and the blue for red.. She turned to him as he blonde hair moved with the wind.

"Who are you?" Taltus asked.

"I'm here to help."

Damos raised his head, seeing the woman and Taltus approaching. He sighed with bitter in seeing the woman.

"Larona?" Damos said. "Where have you been?"

"I've been around. Making sure your actions do not succeed in your merits."

"Larona?" Taltus said.

"Yes. I know you who are, Taltus. Son of Hypernon and Sifera."

"And are you a Titagod too?"

"Titagoddess. One of the first."

Damos reached toward his forearm, sliding the hologram as it reopened the portal. The portal took in Damos and his legion and they were gone from Enigma City. Taltus and Larona remained in the streets.

"I know the Dark God is free." Larona said. "That's why I'm here."

"Do you know where he is?"

"I do not. But this coming battle will require my strength and skill. Negiter is not one to be taken lightly. Not even by Olympians or our kind."

Meanwhile on Mount Olympus, Negiter had arrived. Accompanied by Dyclos and Death. They walked past the servants of the Greek Gods as they were escorted to the presence of the Pantheon. Within the massive citadel of the gods, Negiter stood before the Greek Gods. Each of them were terrified by his arrival. Except for Zeus.

"Greek God of Thunder." Negiter said. "I have arrived."

"Indeed you have." Zeus said. "For what business have you come to discuss?"

"The matter of Earth. What shall be done with it once I deal with their heroes."

"Their heroes are not our concern. Aside from the titagod, of course."

"I already have my lieutenants set forward to decimate the heroes in their own territories. The Titagod you speak of will be dealt with in due time."

"So why come here? Why grace us with your presence?"

"Because the earth itself, is not enough for my conquest. I will require all dimensions to serve under my rule. To join my armies."

"You seek to take this mountain for yourself?" Poseidon asked.

"I do. But I do not intend to rule on this mountain. For a place is already prepared for me on Earth."

Zeus sat and pondered. Staring at Negiter while Dyclos snarled and Death giggled.

"And what will you require for us to agree with your proposal?"

"I cannot deal with the heroes alone. But at once, I can destroy them."

"And you'll need our assistance in this matter?"

"I need your monster." Negiter said.

"What monster?" Hera asked. "For what beast do you require of us?"

"Maybe he speaks of the Dragon Gargoyle?" Hermes suggested.

"Or the Kraken?" Poseidon said.

"Do you want possession of the Minotaur?" Ares asked.

"None of those will do the job. Zeus, you know what beast this battle will require."

Zeus nodded as Hera turned to him with concern in her eyes.

"What monster is he talking about?" Hera asked.

"I will speak to Hephaestus and see what can be done." Zeus said.

"Excellent." Negiter nodded. "I will await the call."

Negiter turned and exited the presence of the Greek Gods. Death's laughter echoed through the marbled room.

14

JUDGEZONE

Sinister Judge operated in the workshop of his palace. Judge managed to obtain a piece of the material found within the Cryptic Zone. Using his scientific intellect along with his knowledge of magic, Judge discovered a way to enter the dimension. The dimension itself was weakening due to the growing power of Negiter. Judge was aware of this information and used it in his workings. Within his palace, he opened a portal into the Cryptic Zone and stepped forward.

Inside the Cryptic Zone was endless energy. The energy within the dimension was absorbed by Judge's armor. As he intended. Looking around as all he could see were dark red objects floating. Some elements of fire, purging of violet rather than the earthly orange-red. A supernatural flame as Judge saw it.

"Intriguing." Judge said. "I wonder if I can use this."

Judge reached for the flame, siphoning the fire into his armor. A bolt of fire came down above him. Judge looked up, seeing Creed flying toward him. Creed landed in front of Judge as the two stood on a bridge. A bridge made of bones. Creed watched as the fire was completely absorbed by Judge's armor.

"You do not belong here." Creed said.

"I've seen you before. I know where. When Judge and Doctor Fortune joined alliances against Spellface, Celd, and that false Conqueror."

"I was there. I aided you and the Supreme Enchanter. What you are doing is outside of the natural order."

"Judge makes the natural order as he sees fit. This fire. This dimension. It's perfect for elemental purposes. Judge can do wonders with it."

"You will not leave with that power." Creed said.

"Judge will do as he pleases. Turn away, unholy one."

"I may be considered unholy by my appearance. But, there is more holiness within me than what lies within you."

"You wish to face Judge?"

"I will stop you from leaving this dimension. By any means."

Judge waved his right hand as the siphoned flame appeared.

"I will use the very power of this dimension to put you in your place."

Creed levitated as his cape opened. Taking much of the space in the air.

"You forget or do you know? I am made of this dimension. I and it are one."

Judge transformed the fire into a flamethrower attack. Creed flew past the flames, swooping around them as he struck Judge in the head with his claws. Judge stumbled as Creed returned, spearing Judge from the bone bridge into a room full of cauldrons. Judge arose, seeing the cauldrons full of liquids, which brightened like melted gold. Creed stepped into the room as Judge snatched one of the cauldrons and threw it toward Creed. The liquid inside had no effect on Creed as he kicked the cauldron aside. Judge exited the room, finding himself in a hallway. He gazed up, seeing the sky spiraling. The colors of blue, red, and gold shined across the air like the dimension's own Northern Lights.

"Judge will not be defeated. I always achieve victory."

"This day, you will suffer a loss. One so terrible, you'll wish you never enter this realm."

Creed's hands eject an axe. Taking the axe, he smashed it across Judge's chest, knocking him across the edge of a ridge. The axe changed its shape, turning into a sword. Creed stood over Judge as his armor began to repair itself. Creed raised the sword.

"Your time has come." Creed spoke.

The sword came down, only to be shot into the wall by an unseen force. Creed turned toward the noise of the shot and was shot instead. The impact slammed Creed through the rocky walls as the wound was bleeding. Pulling out the round, he examined it. Recognizing its form.

"Medieval." Creed uttered.

On the other side of the ridge, Medieval stood. Rifle in his hand. His skull-face shrouded by his poncho. His presence caught Judge by surprise as his armor was repaired. Medieval stood up and saluted Judge before fleeing. Judge, unable to put together the scene, turned toward the opening in the rocks, seeing Creed on the ground in pain. Judge grunted as he turned and walked away. Judge took the Cryptic Zone's energy and began to fuse it with his own power and magic. Opening a portal to return to his domain, another portal opened behind him. Sensing the power, Judge turned to see Doctor Fortune hovering.

"I knew you would come here." Fortune said. "What have you done?"

"I did what I set out to do. I've obtained a source of this dimension's power."

"What for? What do you seek to gain from taking a power you have no understanding of?"

"You should know as much as I. when men like us discover newfound power. Newfound knowledge. We do not turn away. We become intrigued. We learn and we obtain."

Fortune looked to his left, seeing Creed on the ground. His bullet wound slowly healing.

"What do you intend on doing with that power?"

"Preparing for war."

"War?" Fortune questioned. "There's much going on right now than for you to declare war on myself and the heroes of the world."

"The war I speak of is not against you or your kind."

"Then who?"

"Against the powers. The rules of darkness which have been resurrected. I may appear to be a villain in your eyes and in the eyes of your allies. But, make no mistake. The earth is mine to rule and I cannot rule it if it's destroy or taken over by an ancient dark god."

Fortune was silent and still. He knew.

"You know." Fortune said.

"Judge does indeed know and Judge is preparing for the war to come."

"If that's the case, you could come with me and aid us in this battle. There doesn't need to be a war."

Judge turned toward his portal.

"Judge does what he chooses and I answer to no one."

Judge stepped into his portal and stopped, looking back at Fortune.

"When the time comes, Judge will be there on the battlefield. Then and only then, will all the world know it belongs to Judge."

Judge walked through his portal as it closed.

15

A MEETING OF HEROES

Colonel Evan Nader contacted The Resistance as well as The Champions of Destiny along with several other heroes to meet him at the T.I.T.A.N. Headquarters. Upon their arrival, Nader knew of Negiter's growing power and wondered what the heroes had to offer in stopping the Dark God's ascension.

"All we can do is manage locations." Norland said. "Track down anything that may lead us to Death."

"What of Kendrick?" Nader asked. "What of Noldar?"

"Noldar hasn't been seen since Negiter's arrival." Theus answered. "Even my allies back in Eragardia have found no trace."

"Kendrick is MIA." Taltus said. "He hasn't returned to Enigma City either."

Doctor Omega stepped forward. Looking at The Resistance.

"I have an idea." Omega said. "Though, it might seem strange."

"We've dealt with strange matters before." Swordman said. "Another won't be any different."

"Well, have any of you ever time traveled?"

The Resistance looked at each other. They turned back to Omega with no answer or expression to give. Omega shrugged his shoulders.

"Here's my idea. Me and my team will go back to 1875 to recruit an ally we met in the past. He's well verse on these matters."

"Who is this ally of yours?" Nader asked.

"He's called The Lone Outlaw."

"The Lone Outlaw?" Norland said. "You speak of the Hero of Silver City."

"Yes, I do."

"You know of him?" Nader asked Norland.

"I do. Most Canadians have heard the tales of The Lone Outlaw. How he protected the city from foes like Thaine Tucker and even tagged alongside a Death Chaser in his day."

"I take it you'll be coming along with us?" Omega said.

"I will." Norland nodded. "Not every day one can travel through time."

"I will be joining you as well." Theus stepped forward. "I never visited this Silver City during the days you speak of."

"Wait." Jetlash said. "You were around even back then?"

"I'm thousands of years old, young one. I've seen a lot in my time."

Omega clapped his hands in excitement.

"Then it's settled. Me and The Champions along with Flashburn, Commander Norland, and Theus will travel to 1875 to find The Lone Outlaw. Although, we'll need another member for numbers."

Nader turned to the nearby room as the door opened. The heroes looked, seeing a young woman enter. Wearing full tactical gear with her long blonde hair in a braided ponytail. She looked, noticing the heroes seeing her. She stopped. Omega pointed.

"I remember you." Omega whispered.

"What is it?" She spoke.

"Everyone, meet Tessa Balthazar." Nader said. "We contacted her after she had an encounter with some of Oranos' forces some time ago."

"So did we." Ms. Titan said. "She interrupted one of our earlier missions."

Tessa looked at the Champions. She pointed with a smirk as she remembered them.

"I remember you guys. Sorry about what happened a few years back. But, I was on a mission and you were in the way."

"We were on a mission of our own." Omega said. "Unlike you, we aren't thieves."

"First off, I'm not a thief. I'm a treasure seeker." Tessa sighed. "That cosmic box thing, was a treasure from these dark gods everyone keeps whispering about. Anyhow, I've dealt with them before. Easy work."

"You fought against Oranos' forces?" Taltus asked.

"Only a few. Met this hooded guy. It was nothing."

"Tessa managed to obtain an object of their making. Called a Cosmicbox."

"Where is it?" Norland asked.

"Don't ask me." Tessa said, pointing at Nader.

"It's safe."

"How soon do we leave?" Omega asked.

"Whenever you and your team are prepared." Nader said. "What will the rest of you do?"

"I will find Doctor Fortune and a few others." Swordman said. "I'll need them for where I'm going."

"And where are you going?" Nano Man asked.

"The Land of The Forbidden."

"I've heard of the place." Theus said. "Not many travel there and return."

"I've found a way to enter and leave with our lives."

"Theus," Omega said, "If you're interested in going with them, don't mind the time travel."

"What do you mean?" Norland asked.

"By the time we're gone and back, it'll feel like only minutes have passed. It'll be as if you never time traveled at all."

Theus nodded.

"Very well. I will travel to Silver City with you lot and I will return to enter The Land of The Forbidden."

Swordman nodded.

"Then it's agreed. While you guys are gone, I will begin finding my allies for the mission."

"That leaves you and Taltus, Nathan." Nader said.

"I've been researching some mystics. No thanks to Fortune." Nano Man said. "There's a sort of dimension high above the clouds. Said it holds a key to facing dark gods. Myself and Taltus will travel there with some help, of course."

"You speak of the Sky Temple?" Theus said.

"Yes. Have you seen it?"

"Once on my travels. But, be careful. Legends speak of a powerful foe who inhabits the temple."

"We're The Resistance." Nano Man nodded. "We take on all challenges."

"I take it you and Taltus won't be alone." Norland said.

"I'll talk to Rick. See if he's interested in going. Meanwhile, Taltus will travel and recruit two others to join us. We'll need someone of mystic origin to tag along."

Nader nodded.

"Then, it's settled. Everyone knows their operation. Once it's complete, you'll all return here and we'll move on from there."

16

1875

The Spellvector flew through the time-stream. Norland stared outside the window, seeing the warping waves of the fabrics of time moving past his eyes. Theus marveled at the sight as he stood next to Omega, who sat in the cockpit.

"How often do you and your team travel?" Theus asked.

"Whenever we have a mission." Omega answered. "We've been to several places across our travels."

"Interesting." Theus nodded. "Ever deal with other gods and suchlike?"

"Not entirely. But, if we ever had the chance, we would give it a go."

Theus nodded with a smile.

The Spellvector reached the wormhole toward 1875 and the team prepares for entry. All sat down and buckled their seats except for Theus who stood boldly. Flashburn looked at him, seeing he wasn't moved by the turbulence of the travel. Theus looked to him and nodded.

"Everyone get ready." Omega said.

The Spellvector entered the wormhole and the ship buckled. Shaking the team in their seats as Theus levitated himself off the ship's floor to maintain his balance. Within seconds, the ship had exited the wormhole and they looked to the windows, seeing the woodland fields covered with snow.

"Welcome to 1875." Omega declared. "The Northern West."

The Spellvector flew across the northern lands and beneath them, Norland saw horsemen riding down the dirt road. With a moment, he smiled. Omega piloted the ship toward the nearest mountain range to avoid detection from unwanted eyes. Finding the mountain, Omega flew and landed the ship. The heroes stepped out of the ship onto the heavy snow. Such weather was familiar to Norland. Flashburn's heat began to melt the snow around him.

"Looks like the snowstorm has stopped for the moment." Omega said. "That's good for us."

"Where to?" Norland asked.

"We go to Silver City." Omega said. "Find The Lone Outlaw and see if he'll aid us."

"Wait." Jetlash said. "Don't we need a disguise?"

Omega looked over to Theus and Norland. He pointed.

"With the amount of time we have, we don't. Besides, The Lone Outlaw will know it's us the moment we arrive. Let's just not cause any trouble."

Jetlash took Omega's word for it as they tracked down the road to Silver City.

Upon arriving in Silver City, they passed by residents who began talking about The Lone Outlaw's recent events in saving the city. Words of Dodge Town's destruction echoed through their conversations. Omega heard every word which passed through the air.

"Dodge Town is already burned down?" Norland asked.

"Appears so." Omega said.

"Doctor." Theus said. "Where will we find this Outlaw you know?"

Omega stopped and pointed. Theus turned to see a saloon. He nodded. "Quaint."

Before they reached the saloon, a drunken man is tossed out. Stopping in their tracks, they look to the saloon door to find The Lone Outlaw. He approached the man on the ground, stepping on his arm as he reached for his revolver.

"Your days of abuse have come to an end."

The Outlaw fired his revolver, killing the man. Exhaling, he looked to see Omega and his team standing still. Omega waved. The Outlaw nodded before noticing Flashburn, Norland, and Theus. Seeing their choice of attire, he knew they were from another time in history.

"Clint Winston." Omega said. "It's an honor to see you again."

"I can say the same. You're not here to start any kind of trouble, are you?"

"None. I'm here in a matter of urgency."

"How urgent? That Baron back again?"

"Someone worse."

"How worse?"

"Think on a biblical scale."

"That bad, huh?"

Omega nodded.

The Outlaw nodded as he placed his revolver into its holster. He followed the heroes into the saloon. The residents inside the saloon were bothered by the heroes' arrival. Seeing their apparel confused them. Norland nodded to them in respect as they were quickly intimidated by Theus' stature. Winston led them to the back of the saloon where they sat. The bartender came over and left a bottle of whiskey for The Outlaw and he handed him three coins in return. Omega told him everything that is ongoing in the present day. The Outlaw believed it all. Nodding as he drank his whiskey.

"And why have you traveled back to 1875 to face this Dark God? Is there something here that can help you in this matter?"

"Why not yourself?" Omega said. "Or Thaine for that matter?"

"Last I heard, Thaine is doing business in Maverick Town. I expected as much since the Burning of Dodge City."

"I must ask." Norland said. "Is there something here that can help us against Negiter? Some kind of element?"

"How would I know?" Winston said.

Omega reached into his pocket, taking out a pad and pen. He began to draw and showed Winston the drawing. What The Outlaw saw was the image of the Helvish mark. He nodded and thought.

"I've seen this before."

"Where?" Theus asked.

The Outlaw reached into his coat pocket, taking out a mineral fragment. He handed it to Omega. Staring at the mineral, they noticed a red glow emitting from within. Through the small cracks like a burning flame.

"I found that on one of my rides. It was blinking through the entrance of a mine. Yet, whatever it came with was no longer there. All that remained was that.”

Theus looked at the fragment, sensing the energy from within. He nodded.

“I know what this is.”

“What is it?” Omega asked.

“It’s Helvish.”

“Come again?” Crimson Mask said. “What’s a Helvish?”

“Helvish is a word used to describe beings and suchlike from a dimension called Helven. It’s where Negiter lived during his early days. Before his imprisonment. Helvish power is strong. Very strong.”

“That’s the same power we felt when The Specter Errant aided us against Oranos and his forces back in Enigma City.” Norland noted.

Jetlash looked at the fragment and began to ponder a thought.

“I know what we can do.” Jetlash said. “We can use this fragment to manufacture a device to stand against him and his forces. Use his power against him.”

“We could put it to the test. See if it effects those of his forces before we attempt it on him.” Omega said.

Norland stood up at the table.

“Best we get back to the present day.”

“Indeed.” Omega said, standing up. “It was an honor to see you again.”

“Likewise.”

The heroes make their leave, returning to the ship. Behind them, they could hear gunfire. Omega knew The Outlaw was continuing his business. They reached the ship and prepared for takeoff as a wormhole appeared in the sky. The Spellvector took off and entered the wormhole, leaving 1875.

17

THE SKY TEMPLE

The Nano Man and Taltus flew through the clouds of the day. Along with them in the air was Silver Eagle. The three flew past the clouds as Nathan followed a path detailed on a map in his helmet's HUD.

"How far is this temple?" Eagle asked.

"It's not that far. We only need to see it. That's when it'll appear."

"What about the other two? How will they get up here?"

"They have magic. I'm sure they'll teleport themselves to the temple."

The three heroes flew deeper into the clouds and higher in the sky. While they flew, Taltus felt a presence in the sky. A growing energy. He mentioned it toward Nano Man and Silver Eagle and as he did, a beacon appeared on Nathan's HUD, showing the temple. He looked upward, seeing the temple ahead. A massive structure. Floating above the clouds. Silver Eagle paused in flight, seeing the colossal structure.

"That's been up here this entire time?"

"So it seems." Nathan said. "Let's find a way inside."

The heroes flew toward the balcony entrance to the temple. Making their landings, Silver Eagle looked around for the other two who would be accompanying them. Before a word could speak from his mouth, a beam appeared and within it were two figures. Once the light of the beam dimmed, Taltus nodded. The two other heroes arrived.

"The Man Called Fable?" Nano Man said. "Is that right?"

"That's who I am." Fable grinned. "And this is Kang-Zhu. An expert in the field of martial arts and eastern mysticism."

"I dabble where I can." Kang-Zhu said.

"Mysticism?" Silver Eagle said. "You know anything about this place?"

"I've read up on it in the past. It's said that the temple will give its visitors answers to their more dire needs. Perhaps that's why you've come here."

"We need to see if this temple will help us against Negiter and his forces." Taltus said.

"Taltus is right." Nano Man said. "Otherwise, we would not be here."

"Well then." Fable said. "Let's get inside and get our answers."

The heroes stepped forward as the temple doors opened. Inside the temple were detailed statues of dragons. Kang-Zhu knew of the dragon. An ancient being called Astarot. Known in the ancient scrolls as *The Dragon of The Skies*. The heroes continued walking further and once they came to a sudden stop, Fable pointed ahead, seeing a much larger room and within the room was Astarot himself.

"Is that the dragon?" Nano Man asked.

"It is." Kang-Zhu nodded. "That is Astarot."

"Alright then." Fable said. "Let's go and ask this dragon some questions."

"Don't be rash." Kang-Zhu said. "Astarot is very powerful. We should not antagonize him."

"Kang-Zhu's right." Taltus said. "No need to anger the dragon. We're on his turf, after all."

Fable looked at Kang-Zhu and nodded slowly. Kang-Zhu nodded back as they approached the dragon. Stepping forward near the scaly-armored dragon. The height of the dragon was near one hundred feet. Its sun-scorching scales shined like fine jewels. Its eyes glistened with the touch of heated emerald. The six horns on his head resembled a crown in their sights. Astarot turned toward them. Sensing their essence.

"I knew you would come here." Astarot spoke.

"You knew?" Fable asked.

"I know who you are. Who are of you are."

"You know of us?" Nano Man asked.

"I am aware of you. A billionaire infused with bio-nanotechnology. A soldier with desire to be a helper amongst men. A Titagod. One of the first.

A magician who's known to con his targets and a martial artist with much history he knows little of."

"History is not why we've come, Astarot." Kang-Zhu said. "We've come to learn how we can stop Negiter and the Dark Gods."

Astarot sighed.

"There is no stopping Negiter."

"What do you mean?" Taltus asked.

"It is written, Negiter will return from his imprisonment and shall conquer the earth once more."

"But, we can't allow him to do that." Fable said.

"It doesn't matter what you can or can't do. You cannot change prophecy."

"Then, what can we do?" Kang-Zhu asked.

"You must allow Negiter to succeed. To fulfill the prophecy."

"You're saying to allow many innocents to their deaths." Nano Man said.

"Many will die from Negiter's conquest. The earth and all its inhabitants will not. Negiter doesn't desire to kill all life on this world. He needs humanity to worship him. Without humanity, Negiter would have no purpose."

"But innocent lives will be lost!" Nano Man yelled.

"Yes. Nothing you nor I can do will change the prophecy."

"What is this prophecy?" Kang-Zhu asked.

"The Prophecy of the Dynasty Wars."

"I've never heard of this prophecy before."

"The Dynasty Wars surrounds all of Negiter's existence. From his creation in the beginning. His alliance with The ha-Satan. His conquest of Earth to his imprisonment. His release. His second conquest. His downfall. His end."

Nano Man paused.

"Hold on. You say the prophecy declares an end for Negiter?"

"Yes. Negiter will fall at the hands of the returning one who wields The Sword."

Nano Man chuckled.

"I think I know who that is."

"Indeed." Taltus nodded.

"But, before we go." Kang-Zhu asked, seeing the temple shifting from material to metaphysical. "What can we do now against him?"

"Prepare for battle."

"Prepare for battle?" Fable asked. "Are you sure?"

"Yes." Astarot spoke. "Prepare for the Battle of the Universe."

Knowing what they now have learned, the heroes take their leave from the temple. While they make their exit, Nano Man looked back, seeing the temple which was once in his sight, became invisible to the naked eye.

18

THE FORBIDDEN LANDS

Riding out into the unknown region, The Swordman's Sky-Rapier flew across the sky. Inside the craft with Swordman were Travis Vail, Cinderella, and his long time friend, Gozen. The ship approached a vast open field. A fog began to consume the sky as Swordman landed the ship. Walking out into the field, Swordman noticed the mist rising and the fog above. Vail gazed up to the sky, seeing the sun having a rough time peeking through the clouds and the fog.

"Good thing there's no spirits within." Vail joked.

"Where's Fortune?" Cinderella asked.

"He'll be here." Swordman answered. "Right now, we need to put out the signal."

"Ken." Gozen said. "Are you sure we need to do this?"

"The Horsemen are aware of our presence on the land. There's nothing else we could do besides wait for their arrival."

"I do have to ask, why are we meeting with these Horsemen of the land?" Vail wondered. "What could they know that we already don't?"

"I have questions." Swordman said.

"Concerning Negiter and his Dark Gods?"

"That and more."

While they prepared, Fortune arrived through a portal rift. Vail looked at him, sensing the smell of cryptic energy. Vail nodded.

"What happened down there?"

"Judge." Fortune said. "He's taken some of the Cryptic Zone's power for himself."

"And you let him escape?" Swordman asked.

"No. He said he's planning to face Negiter on his own terms. He has no desire to align with us."

"That makes sense." Vail grinned.

Fortune turned to Swordman while looking around the mist-covered field.

"When will they arrive?" Fortune asked.

"Anytime now."

Swordman prepared and within an ear's reach, the sound of galloping caught their attention. Swordman arose from the ground, looking over to his right as did the others. Vail glared through the mist, as the blue flames covered his right hand. The galloping increased in sound and the mist blew past them with a large gust of wind. When they looked again, the mist surrounding them was gone. Only the fog above remained. In front of them, the Four Horsemen of The Forbidden stood. Vail stared at them. Seeing their size and the size of the horses. He nodded.

"Well, I'll be." Vail chuckled.

"These are the Horsemen?" Cinderella asked.

"Yes." Swordman answered. "They are."

The Horsemen in their orderly fashion were Bane, Rider of the White Horse, wielding his bow and arrow. War, Rider of the Black and Red Horse, wielding his sword called the *Redeemer*. Rage, Rider of the Black Horse, wielding his two-hand guns of unlimited rounds. The last one was Reaper, Rider of the Pale Horse, who wielded his scythe named *The Collector*. Swordman looked around, seeing more of the land. He recognized the massive mountains in the distance. He nodded. He knew where he was.

"I wasn't aware this land was close to the Fable Mountains."

"You've come with a purpose, *Myth-Walker*." Reaper spoke.

"I have."

"State your business, Master Swordman." Bane spoke.

"Myself and my allies have come to this land in favor of answers. Negiter has been set free from his prison. His power grows. We need answers on how to defeat him."

"You know the prophecy just as much as us." War spoke. "Negiter's existence is part of a greater plan. There is no stopping him."

"There is a way in protecting the earth." Fortune said. "I am certain of it."

"Are you certain, Sorcerer." Rage spoke. "And are you certain you can survive the coming battle. Negiter and his forces grow in strength by every hour."

"Lads." Vail said. "Hear me out. Why don't you give us a little nugget about Negiter. One we can use in the fight against him."

The Horsemen looked to each other. Their thoughts flowing through the ether.

"The only thing we can give either of you is preparation." Rage spoke.

"Preparation for what?" Swordman questioned.

"For war." War spoke.

"So, there's nothing we can do to stop Negiter?" Cinderella asked. "We're just supposed to face him and what? Let him win?"

"He will win either way." Reaper spoke. "He must win the battle to fulfill his conquest and to set the course of his fate."

"His fate?" Gozen said. "What do you know of his fate?"

"Ask your friend." Bane pointed.

Gozen turned toward Swordman.

"What do you know?"

"You know something about Negiter's end?" Fortune asked.

"I do."

"Please, tell us." Vail said.

"Negiter will fall at the hands of the returning Sword. That's all I know."

"What does that mean?" Fortune wondered. "What does it mean, returning?"

"I do not know." Swordman said. "Until then, we face him. What happens, happens."

Swordman turned away, knowing there was nothing else the Horsemen could tell him.

"Go now." Bane spoke. "Leave this land."

"It is forbidden to the living." Reaper spoke.

The Horsemen turned and rode off into the thick fog. Upon their leave, the mist returned as Swordman made his way back to the ship. Gozen rushed to him.

"There must be something we can do."

"I'm afraid there's nothing else to do but prepare." Swordman said. "Kimmiko, rally all the help you can when you return home."

"I will."

"Me and Cindy will gather our group of supernatural monsters and misfits. We'll need them all for this fight."

"I'll contact Red when I'm back in London. She'll be of use."

"Will she now?" Vail chuckled.

"Don't worry. She's trained for the fight."

Fortune approached Swordman as the others entered the ship.

"You joining us on the ride back?"

"No. There's no time." Fortune said.

"You are correct."

"I'll go out and gather as many sorcerers as I can. You'll do the same on your end?"

"I will. We'll regroup with the others and make our plan there."

Fortune extended his hand. The two shook hands.

"I'll meet you all back at the headquarters." Fortune nodded.

"See you there."

19

HEROES, GODS, AND MONSTERS

On Mount Olympus, a raven appeared and flew toward Zeus, who's standing on the balcony. The raven landed on Zeus' forearm. The Thunder God noticed a note on the raven. He grabbed it as the raven flew away. Zeus opened the scroll and read the writings. He smiled. One of the servants approached him.

"Send word to Hephaestus. It's time."

The servant bowed and went to deliver the message. Zeus stood still, grinning.

Back at the Clark Estate, Kenari sat inside his Swordlair. He prepared for the battle, switching out his traditional sword suit for a more battle-prone one. A fully armored suit. Similar to the armor he wore against Taltus in their first encounter, only without the radiation-laced details. Allison, his wife entered the lair and saw the armor.

"I take it the time has come."

"It has."

"You know I could join you out there."

"Well, I suggest you prepare in case I call for you."

"Are you serious?"

"Yes. We'll need all we can get for this battle."

Elsewhere, Fortune gathered Huang and Tom along with several other sorcerers such as Morhana and Madame LoCasta. Fortune even managed to gain Kular to join them after Atlantis was attacked. In London, Cinderella met up with her friend, Red. Vail spoke with the Ghost of England, telling him of recent events. Creed and Death Chaser appeared before them, sensing the power in the air.

In D.C., Abraham was visited by Visitant Outlander and Dark Manhunter. The two informed him of the growing power. Even the Yonderers were preparing themselves for the battle.

Nano Man, Taltus, and Theus made their return to the T.I.T.A.N. Headquarters. While waiting, Swordman and his wife arrived. Fully armored. After them appeared Fortune, Huang, Tom, Vail, Cinderella, Red, Ghost of England, Creed, Death Chaser, Abraham, the Yonderers, Terror, and Horror. The Champions of Destiny appeared from the sky and they were prepared. Colonel Nader looked at the number of heroes and nodded.

"A mixed multitude in here."

"We're prepared." Swordman said. "All we need now is the location."

The alarm went off as everyone was led toward the large screen in the war room. Nader stepped forward.

"Jessica, what is it?"

"Something's happening." Jessica said, pointing toward the screen.

Nader looked as did the heroes. What they saw on the screen was a news broadcast of the city of Jerusalem. Within the city was Negiter himself in person. He stood in the Old City region. Swordman nodded.

"Well, I'll be damn." Nader said.

"He's finally shown himself." Vail said. "About time."

"He's alone." Omega noted. "Where's his army?"

"Don't be fooled." Terror said. "Those types have armies. You just don't see them."

"What's next?" Nano Man asked.

"We take the fight to him." Swordman said. "The earth depends on us."

20

THE BATTLE OF THE UNIVERSE

Darkous made his way into the Second Heaven, seeing The ha-Satan, waiting. Darkous' shadow cloak moved through the winds as he looked down, seeing the earth and its lands.

"You managed to come." ha-Satan said. "How intriguing."

"Our meetings are no different. You know of Negiter's freedom. Of what's about to come."

"I do. Everything is going as it was spoken. There's nothing we can do about it."

"You know what's ahead." Darkous said. "The Battle of the Universe."

"It's always the battle before the war."

"I know you're infecting the minds of Earth's inhabitants. Even though the prophecy speaks of the ongoing events, this is also your plan."

The ha-Satan chuckled. Staring down at the earth. He turned toward Darkous, towering over him as his six wings spread.

"Our fight is yet to come."

"It is. Michael is prepared for you. As am I."

"I am aware. Although, the prophecy doesn't speak on the outcome of either of you."

"True. That is what we make of it ourselves."

"No matter." ha-Satan shook his head. "I will slaughter you both before my part in this is finished."

"Still high-minded. This close to the end."

Darkous turned away from ha-Satan.

"I will say this one thing, Satan. When the war commences, I will not hold back my wrath."

"Your wrath?" ha-Satan scoffed. "Does the Keeper of the Cosmos truly possess wrath within his being?"

"*The Elohim of Yisrael* will be my witness to your defeat."

Darkous glared toward ha-Satan as he exited the Second Heaven.

Negiter waited in the Old City. He looked up toward the sky with patience. The civilians of the city fled in haste, seeing Negiter within the city. The Dark God did not harm the people. Nor did he attempt to frighten them. He saw them and nodded.

"I wait for your arrival." Negiter said.

Hearing the sound of a rushing wind behind him, Negiter turned toward the Temple Mount and saw the Rapid-Blade. He looked as the heroes appeared from the sky and the ground. Others made themselves known by walking through portals. Negiter saw as he stared down The Resistance, The Protectors, The Yonderers, The Champions of Destiny, and Heaven's Called. Negiter grinned.

"These are the heroes of the modern era?"

Negiter measured the heroes. Each of them in a specific order. The Swordman, Taltus, Nano Man, Norland, Theus, The Unstoppable Beast, Fortune, Voltage, Kular, Tom, Huang, Terror, Horror, Valinor, Emerald, Crystalax, Gale, The Surf, Vail, Abraham, Cinderella, Creed, Death Chaser, Ghost of England, Omega, Ms. Titan, Jetlash, Crimson Mask, Flashburn, Tessa Balthazar, Ambush Bot, and Nonagon.

The Swordman stepped forward, holding his sword. Negiter looked upon the sword, sensing its power. With a nod, he remembered the weapon.

"I haven't seen that blade since my imprisonment. However, you are not The Swordman I once faced."

"I am not. The one you faced is an ancestor of mine."

"I see. You are this era's Swordman."

"I am."

"Then you know why I am here. Why I exist."

"I do."

Negiter looked out at the heroes once more before focusing his attention on The Swordman.

"Your allies are far different than your ancestor. He put his trust in humans. Not petty gods or sorcerers."

"This battle will require all who can do battle."

"Very well." Negiter said, stepping back. "The Battle of the Universe is here and I shall win."

"Advance!" Swordman yelled.

The heroes made their move and attacked Negiter. The Dark God managed to keep himself up, taking the blows from every angle. Even from the sky as Taltus, Theus, Nano Man, and Flashburn made their attacks. Negiter shook his head, forming a force field around him. With his hands, he pressed the field and transformed it into a wave of energy, pressing back the heroes with a great force.

"You believed I would be here alone!"

A loud roar emitted from the sky, gaining the attention of the heroes. From above, Zeus made himself known and Taltus became enraged. Zeus laughed as he presented to Negiter the order of their deal.

"I present to you all! HARMEGIDDO!"

Beaming down from the sky was a colossal beast. Sharing a similar appearance to The Unstoppable Beast, yet its body was detailed in spikes on its shoulders. Horns on its head. Long gray hair. The monster landed on the ground beside Negiter and let out a raging roar. Negiter grinned.

"Excellent."

"What have you done, Zeus?!" Taltus yelled.

"I've delivered the ultimate weapon! Specially designed to kill… you."

Taltus noticed and before he could figure it out, Harmegiddo speared him through the Old City. Zeus fled the city while the Ophfiends appeared behind him, attacking the heroes. Negiter knew what he was planning as he walked toward an open area closer to the Temple Mount and Swordman followed him. The two reached the area and faced each other.

"You know what's to come." Negiter said.

"I do."

Negiter grinned with a very large horrific smile. From his right hand, he formed a sword of his own. Glowing in Helvish energy with the symbol of Helven carved into the hilt. Swordman raised his sword. The two faced off, even though Negiter was three feet taller than Swordman.

"Let us begin." Swordman said.

The swords clashed with a wave of energy emitting from the impact. The wave did damage to the city. Swordman's sword held its own against Negiter's. Both blades were strong enough to withstand each other. Negiter noticed this and punched Swordman. He stumbled on his feet, only to catch himself and slash Negiter's left thigh with his wrist-spikes.

"I have my methods as well." Swordman said.

Elsewhere in the city, Taltus struggled against Harmegiddo. The monster's strength was nearly too much for Taltus to handle. Harmegiddo snatched Taltus by his face and slammed him into the streets of the Old City. Holding him down as he pummeled him with its fists. Nano Man appeared behind the monster and blasted him with his ultrabeam attack. Harmegiddo fell to the ground on one knee as Nano Man flew over to Taltus, looking at him, he saw the blood flowing.

"Oh no."

Meanwhile, Fortune opened portals and dragged the ophfiends into them. Sealing them shut as the ophfiends found themselves floating in a space dimension. Where there was only light from the distant stars. Vail and Abraham eliminated ophfiends with no trouble. The Champions of Destiny and the Yonderers held their own against the winged wolves. The Beast and Kular pummeled the ophfiends in their path. Tearing apart their wings from their bodies. Ambush Bot and Nonagon handled the ophfiends in the air. Melting them within seconds.

Negiter shoved Swordman and swung his sword, impacting Swordman's own blade. The force of Negiter's strength knocked the weapon from Swordman's hand. Before he could grab the blade, Negiter kicked him back. On the other end, Harmegiddo arose and attacked Nano Man, destroying his exosuit. Taltus arose from the rubble, struggling to hold himself together, snatched Harmediggo and punched him through the Old City. With that strength, Taltus fell to the ground in exhaustion. Nathan exhaled with relief, seeing his Nano Man armor decimated within seconds. Norland aided the other heroes against the remaining ophfiends. With the ophfiends now defeated, the heroes turned their focus onto Negiter. Finding him in the open field, standing over Swordman as he reached for his weapon. Norland commanded the attack and the heroes ambushed Negiter. Negiter was only holding back as he unleashed his might upon them. Taking them down with only backhands and kicks.

"I am above your means. I am The Dark God!"

Swordman grabbed his sword and rose up, striking Negiter with the weapon, impaling him with his sword with a heavy strike. Negiter saw the sword in his chest and stared at Swordman. Breathing with heaviness in his lungs.

"It is done." Swordman said.

"I don't think it is." Negiter grinned.

Negiter grabbed Swordman's sword and turned it on him, stabbing him in the chest with his own blade. A strong enough strike, it even pierced through his armored suit. Norland looked, seeing Swordman impaled as Negiter dropped him on the ground. Norland rushed toward him, only for Negiter to kick him across the ground. Negiter looked around, seeing Harmediggo roaring as he fled the city. He smiled, knowing the monster's purpose was complete as he saw no sign of Taltus in the sky. Negiter walked away, seeking to reach the top of the Temple Mount. As he left, Death walked toward The Swordman. Looking down at him as she knelt. She sighed.

"Your life force is fading." she said.

"You would know."

"I didn't expect your life to end… like this. But, my brother gets what he wants. If he wanted you to die, there was nothing anyone could've done."

Death placed her hand upon his cheek. She hung her head.

"I'll miss the adventures we had together. Don't worry, I'll visit you in the spirit world from time to time."

Death kissed him and stood up. Nodding with a sense of respect before she walked away. While Death made her leave, Norland approached Swordman's body. Checking for signs of life as the heroes surrounded him. Nano Man walked toward them as Taltus remained down.

"No." Nathan uttered.

Checking for a pulse as Norland removed his helmet. He searched once again. Norland found none. Norland looked back at Nathan and shook his head. Nathan hung his head low as they knew Kenari Clark, The Swordman, was dead.

Negiter reached the top of the Temple Mount and raised his sword. Taking in the scenery of the city. He savored the moment. Something he's been waiting on for a very long time.

"Now, I take my stand as the ruler of this new era. Of this world."

Negiter took his sword and plunged it into the ground. Quaking the city of Jerusalem. In the sky, portals had opened and through them came his forces of all sorts and the other Dark Gods. Oranos, Dranco, Hadi, along with Death, Noldar, and even Kex Kendrick. Negiter's white cape flowed with the wind as a throne appeared from the ground and Negiter sat and marveled at his work.

"Welcome to a new Dynasty."

WAR
OF THE
UNIVERSE

21

A DARK DYNASTY

Negiter relished in his victory over the heroes and the death of The Swordman. The Earth was his to rule once more. Negiter's Dark Dynasty had begun. With their leave, the heroes took Swordman's body back to Retropolis and his funeral was held. The public became aware of The Swordman's existence and his death. His identity remained a mystery as Kenari Clark was deemed missing. Allison mourned the death of her husband and became reclusive in their Estate. She spent most of her days in the Swordlair training and learning. Taltus was taken to his Fortress to heal from his near-death wounds from Harmegiddo. Nathan spoke with Norland about the recent events, and he couldn't believe them.

"Two of our most bests." Norland said. "One is dead. The other is nearly dead."

"We underestimated Negiter's power." Nathan proclaimed. "That's all. We were outnumbered."

"We had the numbers." Norland responded. "We didn't expect Negiter to be as powerful."

"In short, we needed more warriors." Nathan nodded. "Right now, we need to find others. Recruit them to our cause. Face Negiter again and defeat him."

"How will we do that?" Norland questioned. "The people know he killed Kenari. That has only brought fear upon them. Taltus is out of action. The sorcerers are trying to patch the breaches in the dimensions. The Yonderers are dealing with the rise of more nubreeds turning away from their cause. The other heroes won't face Negiter or his forces in this position."

Nathan looked around.

"Where did Theus go?"

"He returned to Eragardia. To mourn a fellow warrior and to preserve his home from any further invasions."

"Like Noldar."

"Yeah. Like him."

Nathan stood up from his chair. Looking out the window toward Retropolis. In the distance, he can see the sky starting to turn red.

"What now?" Nathan asked.

"Now? We mourn." Norland said. "Figured out what to do afterwards."

"We actually lost." Nathan said calmly.

"We did." Norland nodded. "We lost the Battle. The War is yet to begin."

The ophfiends moved throughout the earth, declaring to all the nations to surrender and bow down to Negiter. The other Dark Gods made their moves across countries. Invading foreign lands and signifying the rule of Negiter. Those who refused were destroyed and their lands became food for the ophfiends. Negiter made his stand as Conqueror of Earth, proclaiming his second Dynasty rule official. Many of the villains had pledge allegiance to him and his rule, becoming his earthly army alongside the ophfiends.

Negiter scattered the lands of the Earth according to the Dark Gods, with each one taking a providence. Oranos maintained rulership over Northern Europe, transforming the lands into a second Blachole. Hadi ruled over the Pacific Islands. Dranco took control over South America, turning it into a land full of destruction and decimation. Death remains next to her brother, Noldar sought out to take over Eragard and with Negiter's ophfiends, he began to plot out an invasion. Kex Kendrick demanded control over the United States and Negiter granted him that wish. Negiter himself, remained in Jerusalem. Proclaiming it the Capital of his New Dynasty. The heroes of the earth went into hiding as the might of Negiter and his forces became too powerful for them to face head-on. The Heroes' Path became silent. Then, there were no more heroes.

THREE AND A HALF YEARS LATER...

22

WAR OF THE AVAGO LAND

Humanity remained under the rule of Negiter. Heroes have nearly disappeared. Villains have become soldiers to the Dark Dynasty. With Negiter's rule going strong, Dranco came to him in regard to the Avago Land. The land itself was plagued with ravaging dinosaurs and Dranco had prepared his army to obtain the land by any means. Negiter permitted this decision, stating the Avago Land had many resources to fuel his rule.

The following day, Dranco led a faction of ophfiends along with his own Ruin Fighters toward the Avago Land, which was set south of the Earth. Upon their arrival, the animals began to become concerned as they fled the open fields. Providing an opening for Dranco's arrival. Once he arrived, the ophfiends took the air to maintain the aerial position. The Ruin Fighters moved into the forest with Dranco following.

"This land, it is more ancient than the ones we've conquered."

Entering the forest, the dark green leaves brushed past Dranco's shoulders, for his height was near the height of several trees. Walking further, Dranco looked down into the dirt, seeing footprints. They were not from animals. He gave a slight nod of concern.

"We're not alone." Dranco said to his Fighters. "Stand alert."

Before he could catch them, Tor-Zar, Sahara, and Kujo bolted from the tree lines. Kujo quickly ambushed the Fighters as Sahara dealt with the Fighters in front. Tor-Zar took care of the other Fighters, before facing off with Dranco. See the Destruction God's height, Tor-Zar smirked, holding his spear steady.

"So, you're the one who's holding our occupation up." Dranco pointed. "You, a little wild man."

"I may be a wild man. But, at least I maintain my home."

"This day, you will choose. Align with Negiter and his rule or die. Not as a martyr, but a failure to your tribes and to your world."

"I choose to die. For I will die with honor rather than serve an evil god."

Dranco grinned. His hands clapped together, forming energy within his palms.

"I am going to savor this moment. I thoroughly enjoy slaying those who do not know their place."

Dranco stretched forth his hands, firing energy blasts toward Tor-Zar. The Wild One maneuvered himself through the blasts, dodging them as they impacted the trees, burning them completely to their roots. Tor-Zar took his spear and drove it into Dranco's left thigh. The Destruction God yelled as he pulled the spear from his leg, seeing the blood. The sight of the blood energized Tor-Zar as he grabbed the spear, having a tug-of-war with Dranco. Dranco annoyed by his injury, slapped Tor-Zar across the trees and out into an open area. Dranco bolted through the trees with a spear in hand. Raising up the weapon over Tor-Zar and the spear came down, only to touch the dirt. Dranco paused, looking around the field for Tor-Zar. He did not see him. Tor-Zar was gone. The sound of the ongoing battle with his Fighters became still.

"What is this?" Dranco questioned.

"Dranco, Dark God of Destruction." said an echoing voice.

"Who are you?"

"You know who I am."

Dranco listened to the voice closely. Hearing the tone and the sound of the words. For a moment, he was unsure. However, he knew internally who was speaking to him.

"Where are you?"

"I am everywhere and nowhere."

"Enough of these tricks. Show yourself."

"And if I do not?"

"Doesn't matter. Face me, Astral!"

"As you wish."

In front of Dranco, dark mist manifested from the dirt, forming a figure. The figure was indeed Darkous of the Astrals. Standing tall. Staring a hole through Dranco.

"We've been wondering where you have been these past years." Dranco said. "Almost as if you abandoned your position."

"How could I have abandoned my calling if nightfall continued. If the shadows maintained their stature. Darkness can only exist when I am."

"You proclaim yourself to be the Keeper of Darkness, yet you do not join Negiter's rule over this earth."

"One darkness is not the same as others. Is the pitch black of the night evil only because it is dark? Can you murder your own shadow and call it justice?"

"Enough of your poetic speeches. I will tell Negiter you've thwarted his plot to conquer this Avago Land."

"I suggest you do. Tell Negiter, these three and a half years, I have been preparing."

"Preparing for what?"

The End Draweth Nigh.

Dranco huffed as his right hand turned into a fist, glowing with energy. He ran toward Darkous with his fists first. He went for a strike, only to find Darkous was gone. Surrounding Dranco was a cloud of darkness. A darkness of great dread. Darnco seeing himself surrounded began to feel uneasy. The dread of the cloud consumed him to the point of fleeing. Dranco and the remaining Fighters fled the Avago Land in fear of being consumed by the cloud. Once he and his Fighters were gone, Tor-Zar and Sahara came out from the forest to see Darkous standing in the field.

"You caused them to flee." Sahara said. "Astounding."

"I appreciate the assistance, stranger." Tor-Zar said. "But I must ask, who are you?"

"I am the Keeper of the Cosmos. I've come to ask of your aid in saving the world."

"I only care for my land."

"If the world is destroyed, you won't have a land to call home. You know this."

Tor-Zar knew he was right. He turned to Sahara, who nodded.

"What must we do?"

23

OUTLAW KINGS

Tarkenania. A kingdom located in the far mountains of Eastern Europe. Its origins mysterious as is its rule. The dark clouds shrouded the Tarkenanian Castle where its leader ruled. In the mountains facing the castle, a portal opened and through it walked Doctor Fortune, Commander Norland, and Sinister Judge. Fortune looked out toward the castle, recognizing it from the grimoires he'd read. Judge stared at the castle, seeing its much larger than his palace back in Judgedath. Norland looked on, seeing bats flying in the sky as the brisk wind moved past them.

"There's something strange with this place." Norland said.

"It's supernatural." Fortune said. "Their leader is of supernatural origin."

"I've heard the tales of this ruler." Judge said. "It is spoken he has lived for centuries. Blessed with immortality from his mentor."

"Who's his mentor?" Norland asked.

"Let's ask him and find out." Fortune nodded.

Teleporting each other closer to the castle, the three made their arrival at the castle doors. Tall structures. The castle was indeed old. The architecture is of gothic imagery. Norland stared at the doors. Seeing the carved images of dragons upon it.

"Do we knock or-" Norland said, as the doors opened. "Never mind."

"Let's find him and talk to him." Fortune said.

They walked into the castle. Within was only silence as the cool air surrounded them. Before them sat a corridor. The floor was made of clean marble. The walls were constructed with volcanic rock. The imagery within the castle was only darkness. A darkness with a purpose. Fortune gazed upward toward the staircase and caught the eyes of a figure. He nodded.

"He's here."

"Follow me." The figure spoke.

Norland, being hesitant, agreed to follow Fortune and Judge to the figure. The figure led them into the throne room where they saw the blood-red chair of its ruler. Dark red carpet covered the marble floor. Paintings on the wall depicted battles of the castle's past. The figure approached the chair and moved his dark red cloak, revealing himself to them as he sat. his long dark hair like the shroud of a wolf as did his beard. His pale skin is near comparison to the moon. His pupils glared like rubies. His body was shielded in armor and leather.

"You've come to my domain. Why?"

"You must be him." Fortune said. "You're Drapels Taryen."

"I am." Drapels said. "And what of my name have you come here?"

"I've heard the people call you, *Vamprevil.*" Judge said. "*Successor of Dracula.*"

"That is who I am. Although, I've never accepted the name of Vamprevil. Such is the people's choice."

"You're Dracula's successor?" Norland asked.

"I am."

"I don't understand. I thought Dracula was immortal."

"Dracula had an end." Fortune said. "He chose a successor for the time appointed and, there he is."

"You still haven't told me of your purpose here."

"We're sure you're aware of what's transpired over these past three years.: Fortune said. "The earth has been taken over by Negiter, Chief of the Dark Gods."

"I am aware of his rule. So far, he has not dared to come to my lands."

"He won't. He'll send someone else to do that."

"Let them try." Drapels said. "I've dealt with many rulers and kings in my time. Another will not make a difference."

"Count Vlados has already surrendered to Negiter." Fortune said. "The Kingdom of Dathlos have already joined his forces and are seeking other kings. You are on his list."

"Vlados has always been a weakling." Drapels scoffed. "He only sought to rule out of power. Not out of right rule.”

“Unlike the past kings, these are Dark Gods.” Judge said. “A simple battle against man will not help you in this war.”

Drapels nodded, understanding Judge’s words.

“And you have come here to assist me against them?”

“We’ve come to ask of your help in stopping them.” Fortune said. “We’re going to take back this world and restore it.”

“I know of what happened before. *The Battle of Jerusalem*, if I recall. Aside from Lord Judge of Centro, it was the two of you, along with other heroes who fought against this Negiter and his army in the ancient city. You lost the battle and in turn, two of your best soldiers were defeated. Retropolis’ famed legend is dead and the Titagod who roamed the skies has gone missing.”

“It was not our intention to lose.” Norland said. “We underestimate Negiter’s forces.”

“Negiter had an alliance with Zeus.” Fortune said. “Olympus sent a monster of their making to ruin our chance at winning.”

“So, the Dark Gods even have the Olympians in their pockets.” Drapels nodded. “This is something I never expected.”

“King Taryen.” Judge said. “Negiter remains in Jerusalem to this day. He will not leave the city for any cause. Dire or not. We can ambush him there and end his rule permanently.”

“With what forces? Can your Judgedroids take the might of a Dark God? Do you have any other heroes at your disposal to clash against his army?”

“We have others around the world.” Norland said. “They’re doing their part in rallying an army. An army big enough to stop Negiter and face him head-on.”

Drapels stood up and walked toward the window. Staring out into the Tarkenanian fields as the moonlight shined upon it.

“I have forces of my own.” Drapels said. “How can I be certain I can trust you?”

“Let us prove that trust.” Fortune said. “It won’t be long before one of the other Dark Gods make their arrival here to take claim of your lands.”

Drapels nodded before taking his seat.

“I will wait for this Dark God’s arrival. Make yourselves ready.”

Meanwhile in Mekeopia, the kingdom is being attacked by Madam Oyu, who's stil lset on becoming queen. Along with her is a man who's strength nearly overpowers those with super-strength. His dark red pants appeared like drenched blood. His long dreads brought fear. His piercing eyes made a statement. He is Rage Killmaster. Known for slaying many armies on his own. They attacked the kingdom with force, taking out most of the Mekeopian soldiers. From there, The Black Viscount made his arrival. Staring at hole through Oyu and seeing Killmaster.

"You still seek to usurp the throne." Viscount said. "Such a sad way to live."

"That throne is mine." Oyu said. "Only I shall have the dominion of this land."

"And yet, with all that has happened, you still intend to squabble over kingship."

"Once I become queen, I will summon the Lord of the Dark Gods and bring Mekeopia under his rule."

"I cannot allow such betrayal."

Killmaster stepped forward.

"Madam, let me handle this false king. I will slay him and you shall become queen."

Oyu nodded with a grin as she stood back. Laughing at the sight. Killmaster clashed his forearm bracelets as he stepped forward. Viscount removed his cape and sword. Holding up his fists for the fight. Killmaster struck first with a right kick. Viscount moved from the strike, elbowing Killmaster in the chest, delivering several blows to his abdomen. Killmaster stepped back, growling. The two went back and forth with punches and kicks. Killmaster relied on brute force while Viscount made use of his swift speed. Killmaster went for a haymaker strike, only for Viscount to leap and deliver a back kick, knocking Killmaster down.

"Yield." Viscount said.

"I am not that kind of man."

Killmaster stood up and walked toward Viscount, only for an energy beam to crash into the ground from above. Oyu looked up to the sky to see Nano Man and Ambush Bot. Oyu made a run for it while Killmaster was surrounded by the three heroes. He would not surrender and before he could make a move, Viscount knocked Killmaster out with a twirling kick to his face. The Mekeopian guards arrived to the scene, seeing Killmaster on the ground.

"Take him away." Viscount commanded.

Viscount turned toward Nano Man and Ambush Bot. He nodded, removing his Viscount helmet as Nano Man's helmet opened up, revealing Nathan's face.

"Been a while." Nano Man said.

"It has. Ever since Kenari died, things have been different. If only I was there."

"It didn't come to numbers. We were simply outgunned."

Viscount understood Nathan's words. Even though, he wished he could've been in Jerusalem for the battle.

"What brings you and the android to my kingdom?"

"It's been three and a half years since the battle against Negiter. Myself and many of the heroes are rallying up a force to face him once again. We've come to ask of your aid."

"And what shall I do with my kingdom?"

"You and your soldiers are fit for the battle against him." Ambush Bot said. "The ophfiends are incapable of combating your Mekeopian forces."

"I believe that." Viscount said. "What of the others? Norland? Theus? The other heroes out there?"

"Norland went with Fortune to meet with some king in Eastern Europe. As for the others, they're scattered across the earth. Recruiting anyone who wants to restore this world and end Negiter's conquest."

"I've studied this Negiter for years. I know of the prophecy."

"And do you think it's coming to pass?" Nathan questioned.

"It already has with his victory. His defeat is only nearing with every passing day."

Viscount extended his hand toward Nathan.

"I'm in." Viscount said. "Contact me when it's time."

Nathan nodded with a smile as the two shook hands.

In another foreign region somewhere in the Middle East, Gozen, Firebolt, and Kang-Zhu traveled across the vast desert to an ancient castle. Once they arrived, they saw the castle was fortified with ninjas and knights.

Gozen and Firebolt knew who they were, Kang-Zhu did not as he stood confused at their sight.

"Who leads an army of ninjas and knights?"

"He's called Lord Na's Me Dru." Gozen said.

"I've never heard of him."

"Many have not. That's what makes him very mysterious."

The knights stepped forward, blocking their entrance into the castle. Gozen showed them a scroll, detailed with an insignia. The knights saw the mark and allowed them passage into the castle. Escorted by the knights, they were brought to the throne room where Lord Na's Me Dru sat. The shade of his emerald cloak caught their gaze. His viper-like eyes gazed up to the three heroes as he stood up.

"And what have we here." Lord Na's said.

"We're not here to fight you." Gozen said. "Only to ask of an urgent matter."

"An urgent matter? You speak of the past three years under the rule of the Dark God."

"I do."

"And what shall I do in this matter?"

"We've come to ask of your aid. Join us as we face Negiter once again. This time, in his domain."

"His domain. Tell me. Do you speak of Helven where he resided or Jerusalem where he now rules?"

"As far as we know, he hasn't made a return to Helven." Firebolt said. "He's been in Jerusalem since he won the battle."

Lord Na's nodded at the information. Taking it in slowly.

"And you require my assistance in this upcoming battle to reclaim the earth?"

"That's why we're here." Gozen said. "Otherwise, we wouldn't have come."

Lord Na's returned to his throne. Measuring the heroes.

"Very well. I will admit, I do not like this Dark God's rule. So far, they've only sent fodder to my castle, asking for submission. I do not submit to foreign rulers. Be them man or god."

"Hold on." Kang-Zhu said. "Negiter sent soldiers to this castle?"

"Two years ago. I refused his offer while others gladly accepted the terms. That is why you see a vast desert out in the distance. Negiter had his forces destroy the fields. Turning them into the sands you saw on your journey."

"But if you join us," Gozen said. "You can restore your kingdom. Restore your land."

"I can and I will. But, I will not join you in facing him. The tactic isn't smart."

"Give us time as we gather more forces." Kang-Zhu said. "We're going to strike him as one."

"If what you three speak of is true, then, we shall see what my actions will be." Lord Na's said, standing up. "Until then, silence is my answer. Now leave my castle."

The knights escorted the three heroes out of the castle, returning them to their horses as they rode back out into the desert.

24

ENEMIES & ALLIES

The Tarkenanian Castle awaited its visitors while Fortune, Norland, and Judge remained inside the throne room with Drapels. He sat on his throne in complete silence. It wasn't long before he could hear unfamiliar movement outside the castle walls. His head raised up, turning toward the window, seeing a foreign army on his land. Fortune looked out and saw the army himself and in front was Oranos. Alongside him was Elizabeth Bathory and Count Vlados.

"Figured he would show his face." Drapels scoffed. "No matter. I wish to meet them face-to-face."

"You sure that's wise?" Norland said.

"This is my land. My kingdom. I will not surrender to a foreign god who does not share my values."

"If we go out there, it will only lead into a fight." Fortune said.

"That's what I desire." Drapels smiled. "What about you, Lord Judge?"

Judge stood silent. His head turned slowly to Drapels. He nodded.

"I am ready for war."

Fortune, Norland, and Judge accompanied Drapels to the front of his castle. The doors opened to the Blacholian forces as they saw the King of Tarkenania in their sights. Oranos stood firm. His eyes widened at the sight of the three others. Bathory stepped forward with a smile on her face, licking her lips. Vlados only sighed at the sight of Drapels.

"I see foreigners have made themselves known." Drapels said. "Where is your decency? Where is your respect?"

"Respect is not one of our traits." Oranos said. "We've come for your kingdom. Unite yourself with Negiter and stand with us. This world is already ours. Why not revel in the victories to come."

"Victories to come?" Fortune said.

"Negiter is aware there are other worlds out there. Dimensions to be taken. Universes perhaps that need conquering. Negiter is rallying up new forces to begin his ultimate conquest. Control over everything."

"That is not possible." Norland said.

"Such belief is common for small minds." Judge said, staring at Norland.

"You wish for me to join your Chief God to conquer dimensions and new universes?"

"It is his will." Oranos said. "There is nothing else."

Drapels nodded with a sigh. He turned his focus toward Bathory and Vlados.

"And you two. You were easily swayed by this false god's promises?"

"Negiter is a just god." Vlados said. "His will shall bring prosperity to all forms of life."

"Joining Negiter's army, I have had a taste of so much blood." Bathory said. "Delicacies one after another."

Drapels gave Fortune and Judge a look before staring up toward Oranos.

"I do have an answer for this Negiter."

"State it now." Oranos said.

"I decline his offer. Tarkenania stands alone. Only I am king upon this soil. There is no one else!"

The ophfiends snarled at Drapels. Oranos' eyes glowed red, looking down upon Drapels. Vlados sighed with bitterness and Bathory growled with thirst.

"Don't be a fool." Oranos said. "Join Negiter and your kingdom shall prosper. Decline his offer and all your land shall be desolate."

"I've made my choice." Drapels said, pulling out his sword. "Now, take your leave from my land."

Oranos with anger commanded his forces to attack. The ophfiends flew with speed toward them, only for Fortune to bring them down with his magic. The foot soldiers ran toward Judge and Norland. Norland fought them with his techniques while Judge did not move. With one look, Judge took out a dozen of the foot soldiers with a beam of energy. Drapels slashed his sword through the ophfiends like a sword through bamboo.

"Bathory. Vlados." Oranos said. "Do your worst."

Bathory and Vlados entered the battle with them both focused on Drapels. Fortune took down more ophfiends and fired a energy blast toward Vlados, knocking him back into Bathory. Norland continued fighting the foot soldiers. Judge was set on Oranos. Staring up toward the dark god. Oranos noticed Judge's gaze and stepped forward through the ongoing battle to face him.

"You are nothing but a man." Oranos said.

"I am more than man." Judge said. "I am Judge."

Oranos fired his Blacholian beams toward Judge, only for the Centronian to deflect them with ease. Startling Oranos as Judge delivered his own set of beams, hitting Oranos in the chest and stumbling him into his foot soldiers.

"One should never test Judge."

Oranos rose from the ground, enraged by Judge's attack. He stood up and ran toward him with a striking punch in mind. Before Oranos could reach him, a blast of lightning struck the ground. Ceasing the battle as all eyes were upon the sky. Through the clouds, the sound of a shockwave was heard. The clouds moved as the coming object crashed into the ground. Dirt blew into the air, blinding everyone. The winds blew and ceased, revealing Taltus, hovering above the ground.

"He's back." Fortune said.

"You…" Oranos said.

Taltus stared at Oranos as the Blacholian god went to grab him, only for Taltus to move with such speed, punching Oranos far from the castle. The ophfiends saw him and immediately fled. The remaining foot soldiers did the same as they all know the story of Taltus from the Blacholian Battle. Drapels descended from the sky, sheathing his sword. The portals opened as the Blacholian forces fled. Even Bathory and Vlados were in fear of the Titagod. Oranos looked back toward Taltus, roaring within his being. The portal closed as Taltus turned to face the others. Norland nodded as did Fortune.

"Good to have you back." Norland said.

"What have I missed?" Taltus asked.

25

THE ANCIENT WORLD

Through the three years of Negiter's newfound Dynasty, The Champions of Destiny with Flashburn and Tessa Balthazar as new members made the decision to travel back in time to witness Negiter's first conquest of Earth. Taking the Spellvector, the Champions went back to the year 100 AD. Upon their arrival in Asia Minor, they witnessed Negiter's invasion. His ophfiends had slaughtered many of the Roman armies. Negiter's might had come without warning. The Roman Empire became his earthly army and they made sure others would submit. Negiter had the other dark gods with him such as Oranos, Dranco, and Hadi. They each took portions of the earth to rule as their own providences.

Oranos had taken possession of South America, entering conflicts with the Mayans, as they did not submit to Negiter's rule. Dranco went and took siege of the lands of Eastern Asia, coming into ongoing wars with the Han Dynasty, the Xionghu Tribes, the Rulers of India, and the Ancient Japanese. Hadi took possession of Europe. Fighting against the likes of the Picts and the Germanic Tribes. Negiter remained in Asia Minor, ruling in the city of Jerusalem while Rome was maintained by his trusted soldiers who guided the rulings of the Emperors in secret.

The Champions fast-forward themselves further through time,

eventually reaching the year 997 AD, where nearly everyone on Earth had accepted Negiter as their rule through the changes in generations. Until a man who dwelled in Northern Egypt named Harold Vosloo came into contact with beings from the stars. They were called The Cosmics. The Cosmics had instructed Vosloo to craft an artifact that would entrap Negiter and keep him imprisoned. Vosloo constructed the artifact for several months in secret. Once it was complete, the Cosmics made themselves known to Negiter and his forces and waged war against him.

The war between the Dark Gods and the Cosmics went on for three and a half years. Vosloo had witnessed the war. While The Champions watched the war take place, they noticed familiar beings involved. Such were a Creed, a Death Chaser, and a Swordman. Vosloo was called upon by the Chief of the Cosmics, going only by the name of Cometor. Cometor commanded Vosloo to bring forward the artifact to the battlefield in Megiddo and once he did, the Cosmics and other gods and heroes fought Negiter and the Dark Gods.

"The end has come to your reign, Dark God." Cometor spoke with an echoing voice.

"No matter the prison you have constructed." Negiter said. "I will return and reclaim what is mine."

Many lives were lost in the war and Negiter was weakened, Cometor used the artifact to imprison him and he gave a prophecy, that if Negiter was ever to be freed, in which it was written in an earlier prophecy that the Chief of the Dark Gods would be imprison and freed, he would restart his conquest of Earth and he would succeed.

"I think we have what we need." Omega told the team.

The Champions made their move as they sped forward through time to return to the Present Day.

26

GODS AND WORSHIP

The Champions returned to the Present Day, quickly meeting the heroes who have made a hidden T.I.T.A.N. Headquarters deep underground. Nader commanded the facility with others. Once the Champions had arrived, many heroes were informed of their return concerning news. Nearly everyone made themselves available. Fortune led the charge as the Champions told them how they traveled back in time to witness Negiter's first conquest of Earth. Taking the Champions' information to heart, Fortune began to assemble units to travel to various sights in learning more about Negiter's plans. Worldly means were no longer an option. Everyone knew their position and their teammates. From there, they left the headquarters.

Fortune, along with Taltus, Flashburn, Morhana, and Maveth had discovered evidence of the Elemental Gods' apparent return. Fortune informed his allies he's dealt with them in the past and knew they would only return to face Negiter in taking the world. Knowing they couldn't allow such an opportunity, Fortune opened a portal into their dimension and the four entered. Seeing themselves in a spiral amongst spirals. The colors shining from blue to red to green to white to silver to brown.

"What are these?" Flashburn asked.

"The colors represent the Elemental Gods." Fortune answered. "They're about to make themselves known to us."

It wasn't long before the Elemental Gods appeared. All five of them in their dragon states. They make their stand before them. Their eyes glaring with anger toward Fortune and Morhana.

"Just like old times." Morhana said.

Fortune stepped forward, his hands in the air.

"We've come only to ask a question."

"State your question, Sorcerer." The Fire God spoke.

"Do you intend on taking the earth from Negiter and his forces?"

"Yes." The Ice God spoke. "The earth is ours to rule."

"I cannot allow that." Fortune said.

"You thwarted our plans before." The Rock God spoke.

"This time, we will ruin yours." The Air God spoke.

"Can we take them down now?" Maveth asked, his firearms ready.

"We see the Titagod has come along." The Ghost God spoke. "Perhaps, he should meet his double."

"My what?" Taltus said.

The Elemental Gods moved aside a portal beneath their feet. The light glowed like a brightening star. The heroes and Maveth shield their eyes from the pulsing light. Unable to see what's happening and with a quick sonic boom, the light evaporated. Taltus looked and saw a figure hovering in front of the Elemental Gods.

"What is that?" Fortune said.

The figure stood upright, wearing a similar uniform to Taltus with the colors of gold and black. The exceptions were an Egyptian Ankh on its belt and the figure was a humanoid Jackal.

"This is Taltus-Anubis." The Ghost God spoke. "He is you, Titagod. From another world. In another time."

"Not possible." Taltus said.

"I am you." Taltus-Anubis said. "I've been summoned to stop your cause."

"Looks like we're about to fight, huh?" Morhana said to Fortune.

"Yes we are." Fortune sighed.

Taltus-Anubis' eyes shined like gold as he raised his arms and quaked the ground. Taltus flew toward his counterpart, with his fists aiming for his head. Taltus-Anubis countered the attack, grabbing Taltus' arms and slamming him into the ground head-first. The Rock God went for Maveth.

The Fire God focused on Flashburn. The Ice God was set on Morhana. The Air and Ghost Gods had Fortune in their crosshairs. The Elemental realm trembled with the ongoing battles. Maveth using all of his firearms to break through the Rock God's hide. The Fire God and Flashburn clashing their flames in energy beams. Morhana used her sorcery tactics to use fire against the Ice God. Fortune could handle the Air and Ghost Gods with ease. He's done it before. Fortune twirled his arms, conjuring a tornado emitted with blue fire. The flames caught the Air God, slowly taking the life from it as he set out to flee. The Ghost God retaliated by summoning spirits from the ground to grab Fortune.

"Not this time." Fortune said.

Fortune held magic in his hands and clapped them, shaking the air, evaporating the spirits with quick ease. Taltus and Taltus-Anubis continued to clash. Striking each other with blows to the head. Taltus fired his lightning vision, only to be pressed forward by Anubis' own fire vision, scorching the sight with its dark blue appearance. Taltus fell back by the power and continued to face him. Fortune looked around, seeing the battles taking place as the Elemental realm began to show tears.

"What do we do?" Fortune questioned.

Meanwhile on Earth, Travis Vail, Cinderella, and Death Chaser approached a hidden vault underneath the grounds of a museum. Entering the rooms, the three find The Mythologists sitting at a table. Their leader, Dr. Geoff Hoff sat at the end of the table, cloaked in his white hood and robe. He saw the three enter the room and stood up. The Mythologists looked over, seeing them and immediately began praying.

"This is a first." Vail said.

"What are they saying?" Cinderella questioned.

"They're speaking in Aramaic." The Chaser said.

"You're right." Vail replied. "But, it seems a bit… older."

"I am not surprised by this visitation." Hoff said. "As expected, you would come to ruin our rites for the Dark God."

"For the who?" Vail said.

"We give alms and praise toward Negiter. The Dark God who's cleansed this world of its wickedness and debauchery."

"Wickedness and debauchery?" The Chaser said. "Negiter is all of those things."

"You are wrong, Soul of Retribution." a voice said, coming from behind Hoff.

Vail looked to see Vernon Lance making himself known. A grin on his face as he stared at Vail.

"Every damn time." Vail sighed.

"Why do we always meet like this, Travis?"

"Because you're always involved in some kind of trouble."

"We aren't causing any trouble. We're only giving obeisance to Negiter. After all, he's worth it all."

"You blokes have lost your minds." Vail shook his head. "You've gone from siphoning powers from demons to worshiping a literal dark god."

"Travis, enough." Lance grinned. "You can't stop us this time. We have Negiter on our side."

Vail looked to Cinderella and Chaser. He nodded his head as they moved back.

"We have someone else on ours." Vail smiled. "Someone you've all met before."

"I will not stand for this!" Hoff said, picking up a sword.

Hoff ran toward the three with the sword pointed. The Chaser swiped his hands, emitting Sinfire as it melted the blade like butter and burned a portion of his forearm. Hoff leaped back in agony, holding his arm as it singed. The Mythologists stood up from the table, grabbing knives from the table and slowly walking toward them. They were not bothered. Lance stood behind the Mythologists, grinning at the sight.

"They will slaughter you." Lance said.

"I'm sure they won't." Vail replied. "Anytime now."

From the ceiling came Malach HaMavet, landing on the floor and with a slash of his sword, he slew the first few Mythologists. The other froze as Malach pointed his sword toward them, yet his eyes were on Lance.

"You dare attempt to threaten me?" Lance said. "Do you know who I am?"

"I do not care." Malach said.

"I am a teacher this world needs. Just as Negiter proclaims."

"You're a disgrace." Vail said. "You're nothing but a Satanic puppet."

"I am beyond a puppet." Lance stared. "I am more."

The lights within the room went out like a gust of wind had entered. Darkness was all everyone cloud see aside from the Chaser, whose supernatural power permitted his vision to see clearly through the darkness. Lance stood still, showing no fear and yet was somewhat concerned. He couldn't see anything, only feel the winds moving around him.

"This isn't either of you." Lance said. "Who else is here?"

"You haven't learned." a voice said in the darkness. "You continue to rebel."

"Who is this?" Lance asked.

"I am the one who brings forth the darkness. Who shrouds the light of evildoers."

"Who are you?" Lance asked, feeling the winds inching closer to his face.

"When you turn off the lights to sleep, I am there. When you close your eyes, I am seen. When you dream, I am awake. When you stare into the thick darkness, I am with you."

Lance, still unable to see, but can feel in the darkness. A presence close to him. A presence not human.

"Show yourself." Lance said. "Bring back the light and reveal your face to me!"

The lights returned and standing directly in Lance's face was Darkous. Lance stepped back in fear of Darkous' appearance.

"You!" Lance said. "Again?!"

"You did not learn your lesson the last time we met, Vernon Lance."

"Negiter will stop you. Negiter will destroy you!"

"Negiter has no power over me. He may be the Dark God. But I control the darkness."

"No." Lance said, running out of the room. "This isn't over!"

With Lance gone, Darkous turned toward the others, seeing the dead Mythologists on the ground while the remaining ones flee the room with Lance. Vail looked over, seeing Hoff taking his leave, in fear of Darkous.

"Seems they remember you." Malach said.

"As all do."

"So, what now?" Cinderella asked.

"Right now, you and Vail return to the heroes. The Chaser has some work to do in the realms. Malach, I need you to accompany Vail and

Cinderella."

"I will, Master." Malach bowed.

"And what of you?" Vail asked.

"I have to visit the Spirit Realm. There's someone I must attend to."

"How? They're dead."

"Even the dead have a part to play in this war." Darkous proclaimed.

27

THE CONQUERED

Negiter remained in Jerusalem, overlooking the city in his own making. The other dark gods roamed the earth in search of adversaries seeking to overthrow Negiter and his rule. While they were away, Jerusalem had a visitor. Beaming down from the sky in the presence of Negiter himself was a figure familiar to the heroes. Negiter arose from his throne to face the foreign visitor. His hands behind his back. His firm, yet emotionless face stared at the visitor. The visitor moved forward, standing in the presence of Negiter and his elite guards. Their armor resembled the Roman Empire, only with slight changes in colors. There was little red. The torso of the armor and tunic were a black as coal. the helmets shined like gleaming onyx. Only their capes were white as snow. They were *The Bellator Nox*.

"Who are you?" Negiter asked. "I've never seen your like before."

"You are the one this world's spoken of in recent years, yes?" The visitor said.

"I am."

"You proclaim yourself to be a conqueror?"

"I am the Conqueror." Negiter said with a grin.

"I do not believe you to be. For I am the Conqueror. King Stroh The Conqueror."

King Stroh stretched his arms and the sky brightened at the presence of his dimensional star craft. The lights of the craft emitted a great brightness over Jerusalem, startling the ophfiends in the air. Elsewhere in the city, Dyclos The Immortal Werewolf glared up, seeing the ship. He growled at its presence, knowing what it meant. King Stroh's hands conjured weapons. Two swords. Negiter scoffed.

"You wish to face me in battle?" Negiter asked.

"I do. How else shall a conqueror be made known?"

Negiter, taking in Stroh's words, nodded. He raised his right arm as a sword of his own manifested in his hand. He pointed the blade toward Stroh.

"You will wish you never came to my world."

The Bellator Nox moved aside by Negiter's command as the two conquerors clashed in battle. Shaking the foundations of the Old City, Stroh's strength proved to match Negiter's own. Stroh's two swords moved with such a speed, even Negiter had to find the right moment to strike. Eventually, he did, knocking Stroh in the chest as he swung his sword. The tip of the blade scratched the torso armor on Stroh.

"Close." Negiter smiled.

Stroh moved with his swords, smashing them both against Negiter's blade. The sound of their battle attracted the ophfiends, other Helvish soldiers, Dyclos, and even the dark gods who were present, such as Oranos and Hadi. Noldar had returned to Jerusalem to the sight of the battle. Intrigued by Stroh, Noldar sat back and watched. Stroh pushed against Negiter, until the Dark God let go of his sword and grabbed Stroh by his neck, chokeslamming him into the concrete. Stroh collapsed into the ground as Negiter's eyes glowed. Stroh moved before the negonic beams could strike him. Stroh retaliated with energy blasts of his own. The violet beams of light reached Negiter, crashing into him as he stumbled back. Shaking off the damage, Negiter looked as Stroh flew into the air and lunged toward him. Negiter waited and grabbed Stroh's arms, slamming him back and forth on the ground before throwing him toward his ship. Negiter flew toward the ship, spearing Stroh through the hull. Within the ship, Stroh's technological soldiers began to attack Negiter. With one swipe of Negonic energy, the soldiers disintegrated. Stroh looked at the remains of his soldiers and Negiter only grinned.

"You may live." Negiter said. "Only if you bow down and worship me."

Stroh threw his swords aside and stood tall.

"I shall never bow down to another. Only I am worthy of obeisance."

Negiter raised his right hand, searing with Negonic energy. The colors of red and black moving through the growing orb. Almost galactic in sight.

"Then, you choose to die."

The observers watched from the ground as they saw Stroh's ship explode from within. Upon its explosion, a wormhole opened and took in the ship's remains. At the throne, Negiter reappeared. He walked toward his chair and sat, sighing. King Stroh The Conqueror was no more.

28

THE SPIRIT WORLD

Darkous stepped through the rifts, entering the Spirit World. Within as he's seen before, were the spirits of those who once lived upon the earth. From the first man to the recently deceased. Darkous moved through the Great Gulf, seeing the spirits above in a realm of peace and below, spirits screamed in agony as they were tormented. As Darkous moved, a spirit approached him cautiously. The spirit, in the likeness of an elderly man stared toward Darkous, realizing he isn't an angel or demon.

"I'm looking for someone." Darkous said. "You may have seen him."

"You speak of the Bearer of the Sword? Yes, he's there."

The spirit pointed upward toward the realm of peace. Darkous knew and thanked the spirit before levitating up toward the realm. Once he was inside, he saw thousands of spirits in peace. Filled with joy. Strange for him as everything appeared bright, only his presence carried a hint of shadow. Darkous looked ahead and saw who he had come for. He stepped closer to the spirit, a man who was in his mid-thirties upon his death. Dressed in a black and white robe.

"Kenari Clark." Darkous said.

Kenari turned, seeing Darkous. He recognized him immediately and greeted him.

"Why are you here?" Kenari asked. "How are you here?"

"I am here for you."

"Me?"

"It is time."

"Time for what?"

"Everything is happening according to its writings." Darkous confirmed. "Your part in this has come."

Kenari questioned what Darkous meant and like a rushing tidal wave, his memories upon the earth had returned to him. He remembered who he was. He remembered what he did. He remembered how he died. Once the memories return, Kenari's demeanor changed.

"Where is he?" Kenari asked.

"Upon the earth. Ruling in Jerusalem as it was prophesized."

Kenari nodded.

"I need to return. I must face him."

"Indeed. But you cannot return to the land of the living so willingly."

"What is there for me to do?"

"You must confront the foe your father once faced. The one who killed him."

Kenari remembered the story. He's been waiting to confront his father's killer for years.

"Where is he?"

"Follow me."

Darkous and Kenari moved like the wind, exiting the higher realm and descending down into a darker portion. Where they stood was Sheol. Kenari knew it from the thick darkness. His vision was rough for he could see nothing. Darkous could see everything. Darkous waved his hand over Kenari's eyes, giving him the vision to see through the darkness. Once he was able to see, he could see the spirits roaming.

"They're everywhere."

"This is the Spirit World, Kenari Clark."

"Where is he?"

"He's waiting for you." Darkous pointed.

Kenari walked through the corridor with Darkous behind him. Through the area, Kenari stepped into an open area. Surrounded by pillars of violet flames. Kenari stepped onto the area's center while Darkous stood back near the pillars.

"Prepare yourself." Darkous said.

Kenari looked around, hearing nothing. The room shook and beneath the ground, the entity appeared. Hovering over the ground as if it had no legs. Wearing a torn tunic with the colors of gleaming emerald and amethyst. Its arms move with the wind. The eyes were golden. Teeth animal-like. It wore a crown upon its head, made of emerald and amethyst.

"King Caprai." Kenari said.

"Who summons me?!" King Caprai screamed with a screeching voice.

"I do. You know who I am."

Caprai glared down upon Kenari. Seeing him as nothing but an ordinary man.

"You have no use to me! I am the Dark God of Magic! I am King Caprai!"

"And I am the son of Kendall Clark. You knew him as The Swordman. You stand before his son."

Caprai paused, inching his gaze closer to Kenari. Looking him in the eyes, he could see the same spirit within him as his father once had. Caprai grunted with anger.

"There wasn't supposed to be another! I became the first to make sure the line of The Swordman was destroyed."

"You forgot one."

"If you are here, you are already dead. Therefore, the line is broken!"

"No. this is all part of a prophecy. A prophecy you ignored."

Kenari raised his hand and through the spirits, appeared a sword. Similar in appearance to the *Sword of the Elohim*. It shined like refined diamonds.

"You seek to slay me! You will not achieve victory!"

"That is where you are wrong. In this spirit realm, I have more power than I realized. This will only take a second."

Caprai raised his hands, conjuring spears above Kenari. Kenari looked at the spears and only shrugged his shoulders. Capral launched the spears, hitting the ground. Kenari deflected them with the sword. Darkous grinned in the distance.

"I will not be defeated!"

"Yes. You will."

Caprai went to grab Kenari, however Kenari leaped into the air, the sword aimed. Kenari plunged the blade into Caprai's chest and stared the dark god in the eyes.

"This is for my lineage. This is for my father."

Kenari drove the sword through Caprai's chest, causing the dark god to convulse and melt apart. Kenari stood above Caprai's remains, burning away like the violet flames around him. He looked at the sword in his hand and turned to Darkous.

"I am ready." Kenari proclaimed. "For I will not rest in peace."

125

29

THE SIGNAL OF WAR

Colonel Nader waited in the T.I.T.A.N. secret headquarters for the teams to return. Jessica appeared to him, telling him to come to the entrance. Nader arrived to see the teams had returned. Somewhat beaten up, yet returned.

"What have you uncovered?" Nader asked.

"We were holding our own against the Elemental Gods and Taltus' Egyptian doppelganger." Fortune said. "But, they left their realm before the fight was over. Something has happened."

"Me and the lot discovered the Mythologists and their leader, Hoff worshipping Negiter." Vail said. "Vernon Lance was there, but he fled at the sight of Ol' Darkous."

"What of the rest of you?"

None have given him an answer. Nader sighed as he walked toward the wall. Unsure of what's next. The doors opened, Nader looked, believing they were found by Negiter's forces. The doors had opened, revealing Theus had returned. Dressed in more armor than before. He entered the headquarters and greeted the heroes and once turned villains. He approached Fortune and Nader.

"Good to have you back." Norland said.

Theus nodded.

"It is good to see you all once again. However, I did not come alone."

Everyone looked and saw what they couldn't believe. Michael The Archangel had made himself known. He greeted everyone in the

126

headquarters. Nader was astounded. He had no words.

"I do not understand." Nader said. "An angel in my presence."

"Michael is here, because it is time."

"Time for what?

"The end no longer draws nigh." Michael said. "The end is here."

"What do you mean?" Voltage asked.

"Theus, send out the signal to your realm. Prepare the armies for war."

Theus nodded and exited the headquarters. Outside, Theus raised his hand, firing a strong lightning bolt. The lightning had reached the realms of Eragardia to which Vindhler, the guardian of the Eragardia Gate had caught sight of the lightning. He turned and blew his horn. The loud wave echoed throughout all the fifteen realms. The call for war had went out. Michael informed everyone to meet with their loved ones before heading out to Megiddo.

Taltus returned to Engima City and informed Stephanie Vale and Alex Havens of the news. He greeted them one final time before heading to Megiddo. The Voltage did the same with his grandmother and friends. Nathan returned to Newark and spent time with Alice Jacobs and Rick Carter. Fortune returned to the Citadel to give details to Tom and Huang, for they agreed to join him on the grounds of Megiddo. Norland contacted his team of young heroes, informing them of the mission. They were prepared for Megiddo.

Back in Jerusalem, Negiter looked out and felt a strange presence over the city. His attention was caught as he summoned Kex Kendrick, Noldar, and the other dark gods. As they arrived, Negiter brought them to his war-room, decorated with weaponry and armor remains of armies he's defeated.

"You feel it just as much as I." Negiter said. "You know this is the endgame."

"What is next?" Hadi asked. "Where must we go?"

"We head to Megiddo. They seek to face us there."

"Who will face us there?" Kex Kendrick asked. "Will it be Taltus?"

"Him and countless others. They're growing an army to face us. We shall overcome them and prevail."

"I heard the call of Vindhler's horn." Noldar said. "This means all of Eragardia is aware. They're on their way to earth as we speak."

Negiter nodded with anger. He detested Eragardians and their kind. Only Noldar did he have a liking towards.

"If they seek to grow an army from across realms, we shall do the same." Negiter proclaimed. "Oranos, gather the forces from the other realms, they will align with us with ease."

"As you command." Oranos said.

"Hadi, enter the spirit world and gather all the malevolent spirits to your side. Their power will be needed in this war."

"As you command, my lord." Hadi bowed.

"Noldar, you know any allies in the fifteen realms that may provide us with assistance?"

"I know plenty." Noldar smiled. "I will gather them at once."

Noldar disappeared before their sight as Oranos and Hadi took their leave. Negiter turned toward Kendrick, who waited for a mission.

"Kex Kendrick, I need you to contact all the villains on our side and those on the outside. Bring them to our cause."

"I can do that with ease." Kendrick nodded.

Kex walked away and entering the room was Death herself, waving at Kex like a child. She approached the table, seeing her brother.

"Where have you been?"

"I've been roaming through the earth. You know, like the other guy." Negiter sighed.

"Then, you know what is about to happen."

"Absolutely! I've been waiting on this for a long, long, long time!"

"Then you shall prepare yourself. We leave for Megiddo at once."

Death clapped with a big smile on her face.

"The time has finally come!"

Back at the T.I.T.A.N. headquarters, Michael informed the humans of what's to come and took his leave. Nader followed him, asking for more information. He only received the same as before.

“May I ask where you are off to?” Nader questioned.

“I will gather the heroes and villains of benevolence and bring them to Megiddo.” Michael said. “I know you will meet us there.”

“I will.” Nader said. “But, with respect. May I ask what’s at Megiddo?”

Michael turned to him. A straightforward look.

“The War of the Universe.”

30

THE WAR OF THE UNIVERSE

Har Megiddo, the land rested until the sky darkened and turned blood red. The winds blew across the land, even the critters fled the location. From the sky opened bright white portals and through them came Negiter, Oranos, Thrudhawk, Domonix, The Bellator Nox, and his ophfiend forces. Making their stand in Megiddo, Negiter was now dressed in full onyx armor with a long cape white as snow. More portals opened on both sides of him and the other Dark Gods. Coming through the second batch of portals were Noldar and many of the monsters and beasts from across the fifteen realms.

Stepping through the portal with him were Arnos the Millennium God of War, Lordi the Millennium God of Deception, Illianna the Millenium Goddess of Sorcery, Emperor Voldor of Svartheim, Deimus the Millennium God of Fear. Even Majino, the Millennium Dark God of Evil made his presence known, standing over everyone on the field for his height was as high as a redwood tree. Noldar turned to Negiter, who saw his army. Negiter was impressed as Noldar grinned.

Negiter turned to his left, seeing Hadi arrive with monsters from the fifteen realms. Fire Demons, Shadow Creatures, Dark Elves, Undead Spirits, Cyclopes, and Trolls. Negiter nodded toward Hadi. Negiter looked up to the sky, seeing numerous aircrafts arriving. They belonged to Kex Kendrick as they made landfall. Exiting the crafts were the Enforcement Order,

Veronica Kal, Minuteman, Mountainrock,   The Ruler, the Exchange Force, the Dominate Trio, the Outband, King Marc, Static Morrison, Deadon the Commando, Kane the Mercenary, Niles Valcrow in his Iron Machine armor, Geier, Bio Man, Jon Cramer in his Nano-Monger armor, Nicolas Jovano, Agency X, Thunderstorm, Abin-Qa, Royal Ghost, Rage Killmaster, Radiation-Skull, The Chopper, Doctor Streak, and Marion von Eldric joined him with Ezekiel McKnight, bringing a dozen Steelers to their defense. Negiter was impressed with the humans who joined his side.

Another portal opened in front of them, this one was darker than the others. A thick darkness to where no one could see. Stepping through with a laugh was Death. Her arms stretched out. A smile on her face.

"We're here!" Death screamed.

Walking behind Death were many supernatural beings that have faced the heroes in the past. Sinister Fear, Jester, Vernon Lance, Dr. Geoff Hoff, Leta, Elizabeth Bathory, Ark The Sea Monster, Lycano, Amazon Jaguar, Quan Hut, Death Raptor, Ink Man, Satanic, Medieval, Mordecai Gascoyne, Balthazar, the Plague Doctors, and many spirits. Death danced at their arrival. Beaming through the sky with great wings was The ha-Satan himself. Looking down at the field, seeing the forces gather.

"It is time."

Along with him, coming up through the ground were both Demonticronto and Adrambadon. They make their allegiance with Negiter. For his rule brought them both great power. Death approached Negiter, looking at his armor. She nodded with a grin.

"So, what's next?" Death asked.

"Now, we wait for them." Negiter said.

The silence grew upon the land as the blood red sky continued to gloom. In front of them at a distance, the sound of a great boom cracked. Gathering their attention. Negiter looked on, seeing a rift open. Through the rift arrived Doctor Fortune, Doctor Mysticism, Huang, Morhana, Violetress, The Voltage, Kular, Travis Vail, Gabriel Abraham, Cinderella, Red, Creed, Death Chaser, Papa Afterlife, Fable, even the Yonderers had come with them. Terror, Jade Horror, Emerald, Crystalax, Valinor, Lois Frost, Magic Carpet, Gale, Holygoblin, and The Surf. Even the Atlantean armies arrived on the battlefield. Negiter scoffed at their arrival. Another thunder-like sound came from above, Negiter stared into the sky as Taltus, Larona, Nano Man, Silver Eagle, Ambush Bot, Nonagon, and Bionic Rage arrived. Nano Man landed on the ground, armored in his Godhunter Armor. Detailed with the colors of midnight teal, gold, and silver layered throughout the armor.

From the sky nearby also came the Spellvector with the Champions of Destiny onboard with Norland, Flashburn, Tessa Balthazar, Jack Stone, Dante Hale, Devil-Knight, Q-Arrow, Cry-Slasher, Shadow Hardy, Kang-Zhu, Gozen, Firebolt, Cheeseburger Man, and even The Lone Outlaw had arrived. The heroes made their stand against Negiter and his forces. Both sides staring each other down. Behind the heroes arrived Theus with armies from Eragardia and their allies. Lady Soya, The Mighty Trio, The Light Elves, The Knights of Shadoheim along with their leader, the Wraith Knight. Even the Black Viscount arrived with his own ship and Mekeopian knights.

"He brought an arsenal." Nano Man said.

The Lone Outlaw looked around the battlefield, seeing Negiter's army in the distance. He looked at the sky and the scenery of the landscape. He turned to Omega.

"So, this is the future?"

"More or less." Omega shrugged. "I've seen beyond this point. Hell, I'm from beyond this point."

Both sides were set as they stared. Negiter gazed up, seeing The ha-Satan hovering on his side. Looking toward the heroes, he saw no one. Negiter smiled.

"We have the victory." Negiter said.

"Of course, we do." Death said. "They have no protector over them."

It didn't take long as a lightning bolt shot through the sky, hitting the ground in front of the heroes. Catching everyone's attention. From the ground arose the Mutant-Thing, the Restoration Man, and the Ghost of England. Above the heroes with a quick flash of light manifested both the Visitant Outlander and Dark Manhunter. With them, shrouded in darkness came Beatrice and Darkous himself. Darkous looked forward, seeing The ha-Satan in his sights.

"It is time." Darkous said.

Negiter raised his sword.

"This day, we shall prevail!" Negiter yelled. "This day, this world and this universe, is ours!"

The Dark Forces yelled as they charged toward the heroes. Doctor Fortune looked on, turning back to Theus, Nano Man, and the others. He nodded.

"This is the day. It is time."

The heroes made their charge, pacing toward the Dark Gods. The armies clashed in combat, shaking the foundations of the earth. The ha-Satan remained in the sky as did Darkous. Neither one made a move as the war took place beneath them. The Voltage moved with speed, bolting through the malevolent spirits in his sight as Nano Man charged them with his armor's increased power. The light and dark elves clashed in battle, continuing an eternal conflict. The field was covered in war. Every direction was a battle. Creed fought through a series of demons before catching sight of Medieval.

"You believed it was over?" Creed said.

"This is what I wanted!" Medieval yelled.

Creed dodged Medieval's rifle shots, inching closer toward him. As Creed reached for Medieval's neck, Medieval raised a shotgun, blasting Creed in the chest. Medieval turned as Maveth clashed him with his sword.

"You have might." Medieval said.

"You have no honor." Maveth replied.

The Voltage moved throughout the battlefield, taking out the opposing forces. Through his quickening speed of lightning, he paused to see King Marc standing before him, holdiing up his staff.

"Our battle is not over!" King Marc yelled.

"Oh boy." Voltage said sarcastically.

King Marc went to stab Voltage with the spear, Voltage leaped over him, knocking the staff from his hand and kicking him into the ongoing battle between the Elves. Within the fighting, Marc was overtaken by the Elves, both light and dark. Voltage chuckled before going elsewhere on the field.

Nano Man flew around and saw his enemies on the field, waiting for him. Bio Man smashed his fists together while Iron Machine and Nano-Monger began conjuring plans for Nathan's demise. Hearing the talking, Nathan could only sigh with annoyance.

"These guys, again?"

"I'll handle them." Wraith Knight said.

Wraith Knight sent his army to combat Nano Man's adversaries, quickly defeating them. Nano Man nodded and waved.

"Thanks, man. Cool armor."

Theus flew across the air, clashing against Emperor Voldor. Smashing him with his lightning strike, Theus looked around, seeing Noldar and Illianna facing the heroes. Theus landed in front of them, his hands covered in lightning. Noldar grinned.

"We're doing this battle again?" Noldar said.

"Appears we are." Theus said. "Leave Illianna before it's too late."

"It's already too late." Illianna smiled. "This is where I belong."

"Your loss."

Illianna started conjuring magical whips from the ground. She went to strike Theus, suddenly being attacked by Lady Soya while the Mighty Trio fought against the other forces Noldar brought. Behind Theus came Arnos and Lordi. Theus sighed.

"Remember what happened the last time we fought?" Theus said.

"This isn't the last time." Arnos said. "Look around you. We have an army on our side!"

"As do I."

Arnos and Lordi rushed toward Theus. The Millennium Thunder God, using his might, fired a massive bolt of lightning into the ground, causing the ground itself to bolster up, knocking Arnos and Lordi into the air, only to be taken down by The Beast, leaping through the air.

Theus smiled and turned around, feeling the ground quaking by footsteps. He turned, seeing Majino coming toward him. His roars echoed the sound of burning waves. Theus smiled.

"This day has long been overdue." Majino said.

"I've heard the tales of your feats." Theus said. "Now, I can see if they were true."

Theus bolted through Majino's chest. Smashing through him with his increased lightning. Majino was not bothered as eh grabbed Theus by his legs and slammed him into the ground. Norland took down many of Marion's V.A.U.L.T. soldiers as Nano Man stood next to him.

"Who's next?" Norland said.

The two heroes turned around to see The Thetan, Xeno, and Black Sector waiting for them both. Nano Man sighed yet again.

"Those two friends of yours?" Norland asked.

"Not exactly. More like people I've pissed off over time. What about the Native? Yours?"

"Yeah. Somewhat."

"You remember what you did to us?" The Thetan said.

"I do." Nano Man joked. "I'm about to do it again."

Thetan fired a blast of energy along with Xeno toward Nano Man, causing him to fly into the air. Black Sector stared at Norland, remembering their first encounter. Norland nodded as his hands were covered in ice.

"I see the Lord Blizzard remains with you." Sector said.

"He does. Which is why I won't lose today."

"Don't be sure of yourself. Or his might."

The Bellator Nox used their might to defeat many of the Atlanteans, only to be ambushed by a Horde of vampires and behind them came Drapels, moving like a giant bat across the battlefield. Negiter saw him and anger kindled within him.

In the sky, Darkous and ha-Satan inched closer to one another as the beating echoes of weapons and explosions sounded from below. Satan savored the ongoing war while Darkous remained stoic.

"This is the day you've waited for." ha-Satan said. "The day you could face me without any penalty to your actions."

"Today is that day. However, things will go unexpected for everyone here."

"Only thing happening this day is your death. By my hand."

Darkous stretched his arms, conjuring a great shadow behind him. His pupils shifted from white to red.

"Here's your opportunity, Morningstar."

Darkous and Satan clashed in battle, creating a great thunder in the sky. Fortune looked up as did Norland and Nano Man, seeing the two battling.

"What is happening?" Norland asked.

"It seems Darkous and Satan himself are clashing in battle." Fortune said. "Just as we knew would happen."

Darkous slammed his fists in Satan's head. Satan rolled through the air, catching his balance. Darkous flew toward him with his hands open, looking to grab Satan. Satan dodged the coming grab, kicking Darkous to the ground. On the ground, Darkous rose up, seeing Beatrice running toward him. Darkous raised his hand, stopping her.

"Help the heroes." Darkous said. "Satan is mine."

The war continued with many entities dead. Some spirits vanishing from the fights. Hadi moved through the heroes. Only to find herself confronted by The Unstoppable Beast, who came down from the sky. He roared in her face before grabbing her by the throat and spearing her through many of Negiter's forces. Negiter grunted with anger. Kendrick saw The Beast and turned to Mountainrock.

"Remember why you're here." Kendrick said.

Mountainirock, Amazon Jaguar, and The Ruler ran toward The Beast. The Beast, seeing them let out a great roar as he charged toward them with no fear. Jack Stone and Dante Hale made easy work of Static Morrison and Deadon the Commando. Kane The Mercenary attempted to get a quick shot at Hale, only for Stone to rush him with a quick punch, knocking him out with ease. The Mutant-Thing and Dyclos fought one another. Dyclos moved with speed, passing through Mutant-Thing's growing pillars. Dranco made his own stampede, pummeling through the forces. Savoring the moment as he laughed with joy. The Voltage aided Gozen, Firebolt, and Kang-Zhu against the returning might of the Warriors of the Claw.

"When will these guys just stop." Voltage sighed.

Voltage went to approach the heroes, only to be knocked down by a hydro blast. Looking up, he saw Sonicwave running toward him. Voltage stood up for the fight, only for Sonicwave to be knocked down by General Rilla.

"This is no favor to you." Rilla said.

"Whatever you say, man."

Rilla had arrived and his Fellowship was with him. The Yonderers looked on as Rilla joined their side, fighting against Negiter's forces.

"Nubreeds shall prevail this day!"

Rilla easily defeated many dark elves and fire demons in his path as Terror approached him while shooting many more demons in his path.

"Why are you on our side?" Terror asked.

"Because. With Negiter in charge, many nubreeds will have no peace. I do this for them. Not for these heroes and their cause."

Terror only nodded and returned to the fight as did Rilla. The Enforcement Order teamed with the Exchange Force to take down the Champions. A battle which did not last as the Champions had the Yonderers and Rilla's Fellowship on their side. The Steelers made their move toward the Yonderers and the Fellowship.

"He made more!" Rilla screamed. "Humans and their toys."

Charging up his energy, Rilla blasted the Steelers, breaking apart their bodies before turning them into electrified weapons. Meanwhile, Vail, Abraham, Cinderella, and Red fought off the fire demons. Waiting for them was Leta and Vernon Lance. Vail looked at them both and could only shake his head.

"I've had enough of these two." Vail sighed.

"Let's end it here." Cinderella said.

Cinderella and Red ran toward Leta as Vail fought Lance in a fistfight. No supernatural powers used. The Death Chaser moved through the field with ease, burning most of the ophfiends into cinders. Majino continued to pummel Theus until Taltus arrived and punched the Dark God, knocking him to the ground. Theus arose as Majino fell.

"I could've taken him." Theus said.

"Didn't look like you were."

Fable and Balthazar clashed in a battle of magic. To the point of Fable, using his con-artist techniques to manipulate Balthazar into trapping himself in an alternate dimension. Fable shrugged his shoulders, seeing it as an easy win. Fable turned to his right as Sinister Fear approached him, conjuring smoke to instill fear. Fable, looking at the smoke, inhaled it.

"What are you doing?" Sinister Fear said.

"Dude, this stuff is wack!" Fable said. "I've dealt with better fragrances."

Devil-Knight found himself facing Sinister Fear and Jester once more. Fighting against them at once, Norland came through, taking out Jester. Negiter easily took out many of the Eragardia forces. Turning around to find himself facing against Sinister Judge.

"You." Negiter said. "You could've joined me and had what you desired."

"You took what I desired most." Judge said. "This world is mine to rule!"

Judge blasted Negiter, knocking him to the ground. Cheeseburger Man ran through the battlefield, avoiding any conflict that may appear. From falling bodies of ophfiends to dead demons. He came to a stopping point as he saw The Chopper.

"Not again!" Cheeseburger Man screamed.

The Chopper ran toward him with his cleaver. Cheeseburger Man smiled as he took out his two guns of ketchup and mustard, shooting The Chopper in the face with them. Blinding him as he made his escape. Black Viscount and Rage Killmaster had their rematch, with Viscount taking down Killmaster with ease. Learning his tactics after their first encounter, Viscount knew what to do in order to win.

Judge held Negiter down with more blasts of energy. Negiter knew the energy wasn't from the earth as Judge's eyes began to glow golden, similar to Creed. Judge had weaponized the Cryptic Zone's energy. Adrambadon sensed the energy and flew over to Negiter's defense, only for Judge to take down Adrambadon with his own dimension's energy.

"I am not a fool. I am Judge."

Demonticronto speared Judge from behind, aiding his allies. Judge rose up, staring at the three entities.

"I've conjured demons of my own. I fear no gods."

Demonticronto and Adramadon were shoved back by Fortune, Mysticism, and Huang. Fortune approached Judge.

"You came." Fortune said.

"Judge does what he chooses."

"Of course."

Elsewhere on the battlefield, Kex Kendrick fought off many Eragardian soldiers and looked toward Doctor Streak, seeing him staring at everyone on the battlefield.

"Streak! Now is your time!"

Streak nodded and put himself in a running stance, combing his hair back. Within a second, Streak was gone and many of the heroes' allies with him. . Their bodies became nothing more than torn flesh electrified. He came to a stop, only to be speared by Rapidshine, who moved faster than he could imagine. Violetress used her magic, helping Malach, Tom, and Huang against the Blacholian forces. The Lone Outlaw walked through the battlefield, shooting every demon that came across him. Stopping in his tracks as he saw Medieval. Medieval looked at him and his revolver.

"Let's do this your way." Medieval said, preparing a move.

Outlaw nodded, Medieval pulled out his own and stood in a duel-like stance. Outlaw, knowing what's to come did the same. Before they could fire, Vail ran toward him, holding a revolver of his own.

"Use this one." Vail said, handing Outlaw a revolver.

Outlaw looked at the revolver, seeing its peculiar design. An insignia was stamped on the handle. An insignia of the letter H attached to the number seven within a circle. Vail nodded.

"Got it from a place far from here on an accidental visit. It'll be of good use."

The Outlaw and Medieval prepared themselves and took the shots. Medieval's gunfire, but the force of the bullet in the revolver which Outlaw held managed to pierce through Medieval's round, hitting him in the chest, killing him permanently. Outlaw walked over and looked at him. Creed appeared on the side, looking at Medieval.

"He's finally gone." Creed said.

"He is." Outlaw nodded.

Thunderstorm struck the ground with his own lightning bolts. Hitting many of the heroes' forces. Behind Theus arrived and slammed him with his own lightning bolt.

"You may use its power, but I am the beholder of it." Theus proclaimed.

The Plague Doctors came together and began to recite a spell. Hearing the sound of their speech and sensing the power growing beneath the ground, Larona flew through the Doctors, knocking them apart and breaking the spell. In the air, Darkous and Satan continued their battle. Satan, getting the upper hand struck Darkous, knocking him to the ground, shrouding the battlefield in darkness. Satan looked down and grinned. But, above him, Michael made himself known.

"I should've known." Satan said.

"You already knew. For it is written."

Terror and Horror stood on the battlefield, seeing their demonic doppelgangers had returned. Standing with Rorret and Rorroh was the demonic counterpart of Travis Vail, Liav Sivart. Vail looked and saw his doppelganger and sighed once again, approaching Terror and Jade.

"You know what to do?" Vail asked.

"We do." Terror said.

"Let's get to it." Vail smiled.

Terror and Horror raised their firearms, shooting their counterparts once again as Vail conjured his blue flames to scorch his counterpart. Their bodies laid on the ground as Drapels' vampire Horde rushed over to consume them. Visitant Outlander walked the battlefield as ophfiends went to strike him, Outlander held his hand, freezing the flying the creatures. Glaring deep into their eyes.

"Do you know who I am."

Outlander balled his fists and exploded the ophfiends. Meanwhile, the Yonderers and Fellowship took out most of the fire demons and dark elves. The Steelers were defeated as Rilla found McKnight, hiding in the rubble. Rilla grabbed him by his throat, levitating into the air.

"You created those abominations."

"Your kind are a disgrace. A virus to our world. You all must be eradicated"

"You speak of evil, yet you express it through your actions. No matter. You may join them in death."

Rilla squeezed McKnight's neck, exploding him by decapitation. McKnight's body fell to the ground as some of the demons began feasting on it. Rilla watched on in disgust, blasting the demons into ash with his electromagnet beams. Ink Man conjured his tattoos on the battlefield, clashing against Death Chaser and Creed. Quan Hut and Death Raptor went and fought against Dante Hale and Ghost of England. The Restoration Man snatched many ophfiends into the ground, spitting out their bones. The Death Raptor swooped over Hale, scratching his face. Turning around, the Death Raptor went for another strike, only to be taken down by Devil-Knight's daggers.

Michael and Satan fought in the air with thunder following their strikes. Satan maneuvered Michael's sword swipe and kicked him to the ground. Negiter looked on, seeing the battle slowly coming to an end. His eyes glow red as he rushed through the heroes. Theus watched, seeing Negiter's inner rage growing. Norland also saw it.

"What now?" Norland asked.

"There's one more thing." Theus grinned.

Behind Negiter came down The Demolisher, an automaton from

Eragardia. The Demolisher struck down Negiter with an energy beam. Negiter rose up and chokeslammed The Demolisher.

"Foolish machine."

Negiter took a turn and in front of him appeared the Specter Errant, brightening the battlefield.

"I know you." Negiter said, seeing the Helvish mark.

"And I know you."

Specter Errant blasted Negiter with his own energy. Driving Negiter into the dirt. Negiter attempted to fight back, but his own power was too strong to combat. Noldar went to run as Theus stopped in front of him.

"Come on, Theus. The war is over as you can see. Let me pass."

"No."

Theus took his fist and punched Noldar, knocking off his helmet and knocking him out. Theus shook his head as he looked down upon Noldar.

Specter Errant and Darkous held down Negiter with their power, digging him deeper into the ground. Negiter struggled to retaliate, for his strength was diminishing. He looked up to the sky in fear, seeking aid from Satan himself.

"Now!" Negiter yelled, stretching his hand out.

Satan smiled and clapped his hands, causing a great distress on the battlefield, knocking down everyone. The Demolisher froze and Negiter arose, shoving the automaton to the ground. Negiter looked up toward Satan and nodded. Taltus rose up from the ground, seeing everyone down. Nano Man hovered up as Norland and Theus also stood up. Even The Beast rushed from the debris around him. Negiter noticed his armor was breaking and grunted in annoyance.

"It's up to us." Norland said.

"Indeed." Theus said.

"Well then," Nano Man said. "Let's get it done."

The Resistance stepped forward toward Negiter. The Dark God saw them and breathed. As they faced each other, Satan descended beside Negiter.

"Is that The Devil?" Nano Man said.

"It is." Theus said.

"Ready to cleanse this world?" Satan asked Negiter.

"I am."

The Resistance fought against Negiter and Satan and were no match. Satan easily outmatched them in might while Negiter pummeled The Beast into the dirt. The heroes were down. Satan only laughed.

"This war is ours!" Satan yelled.

"No." Darkous said, behind them. "It is not."

Darkous opened his hands, revealing a bright flash of white light. The light emitted greatly, blinding both Negiter and Satan. The sky suddenly changed from blood red to a violet-white mixture. The thunder cracked above with an even greater strength. Lightning struck from all sides. In the sky, the clouds opened to unveil a figure. Both sides glared up to the clouds, seeing only a silhouette of a hooded figure, wielding a sword.

"Is it?" Nano Man said.

The figure appeared before them as The Swordman. Dressed in his traditional uniform, only this time was all white. The Swordman descended on the ground, nodding toward Darkous. Dyclos ran toward The Swordman, only to be struck down by his blade. Dranco made his move, quickly decapitated by The Swordman. Satan stared at The Swordman, feeling the spiritual nature over him.

"I can't. I can't be here any longer."

Satan went to flee until Darkous grabbed him by his legs. Michael flew over and grabbed his arms. On the ground nearby, a sinkhole had opened and they tossed Satan into the hole, falling into the bottomless pit. Negiter stood alone for Death and Hadi had fled. Negiter raised his sword toward The Swordman.

"I will win this day or die as a conquer."

"Your choice is already made." The Swordman said. "Now, come and face me."

Negiter ran toward Swordman. The two clashing their blades until Swordman moved, striking Negiter in his chest. Swordman took his sword and impaled Negiter. Stumbling in his steps, Negiter collapsed. The Swordman stood over him and nodded.

"Your Dynasty is no more."

Negiter was dead. The War was over. The Resistance looked over to Swordman, nodding. The Swordman nodded back, sheathing his sword.

"We won." Norland confirmed.

EPILOGUE

One Year Later.

Crime has decreased throughout the world. The heroes have returned to their duties. The villains have disappeared in many parts of the world. A sense of peace had come over the world. Taltus continued to watch over Enigma City. Commander Norland led a new faction of heroes for T.I.T.A.N. The Yonderers and the Fellowship began to work together to ensure nubreed safety. Nathan Hawke married Alice Jacobs in Newark. Theus had been crowned King in Eragardia. Travis Vail continued his occult detective work, working alongside more allies in the field.

In Retropolis, many sought out The Swordman, but had never seen him since his death.

Atop the skyscraper of Retropolis, The Swordman looked over the city. Still in his new white attire. Darkous appeared toward him, only nodding before vanishing through a dark mist. What he saw was peace. From now on, The Swordman will remain a hidden light amongst the living.

FINAL WORDS

A THANK YOU TO THOSE WHO HAVE FOLLOWED THIS SERIES SINCE ITS BEGINNING ON MARCH 6, 2018. THE HEROES AND VILLAINS' JOURNEYS HAVE COME TO AN END.

THE LITERARY DARK TITAN UNIVERSE IS OFFICIALLY CONCLUDED.

HOWEVER, WITH THE END OF ONE UNIVERSE, ANOTHER IS BORN.

FOR NOW, CLOSE THE BOOKS AND KEEP YOUR EYES ON THE SCREENS.

- *TY'RON W. C. ROBINSON II, CREATOR/AUTHOR*

ABOUT THE AUTHOR

Ty'Ron W. C. Robinson II is the author of several works of fiction. Including the *Dark Titan Universe Saga* series, *The Haunted City Saga* series, EverWar Universe Literature, Symbolum Venatores, and more. More information pertaining to the literary works of the Universe of Realms can be found at darktitanbooks.com.

FOLLOW DARK TITAN PUBLISHING
X/Twitter: @DarkTitanBooks
Instagram: @darktitanbooks
Facebook: @darktitanpublishing
Threads: @darktitanbooks
TikTok: @darktitanbooks

www.ingramcontent.com/pod-product-compliance
Lightning Source LLC
Chambersburg PA
CBHW051833130726
47987CB00002B/532